GABRIEL'S JOURNEY

ALISON HART

PEACHTREE
ATLANTA

Ω

Published by
PEACHTREE PUBLISHERS
1700 Chattahoochee Avenue
Atlanta, Georgia 30318-2112
www.peachtree-online.com

Cover design by Loraine M. Joyner
Book design by Melanie McMahon Ives

Photo credits: pp. 155, 157, 160, 161, and 162 courtesy of the Library of Congress

Printed in December 2010 in Bloomsburg, PA, by RR Donnelley
United States of America
10 9 8 7 6 5 4 3 2 1 (hardcover)
10 9 8 7 6 5 4 3 2 1 (trade paperback)

Library of Congress Cataloging-in-Publication Data

Hart, Alison, 1950-
  Gabriel's journey / by Alison Hart.-- 1st ed.
    p. cm.
  Summary: Thirteen-year-old Gabriel, a former slave, leaves behind his life as a professional jockey and joins his father in the Fifth U.S. Colored Cavalry at Camp Nelson, Kentucky.
    ISBN-13: 978-1-56145-442-6 / ISBN-10: 1-56145-442-7
    ISBN-13: 978-1-56145-530-0 / ISBN-10: 1-56145-533-X
  1. United States--History--Civil War, 1861-1865--Juvenile fiction. [1. United States--History--Civil War, 1861-1865--Fiction. 2. Soldiers--Fiction. 3. Horses--Fiction. 4. African Americans--Fiction. 5. Freedmen--Fiction. 6. United States. Army. Cavalry--Fiction. 7. Camp Nelson (Ky.)--History--19th century--Fiction. 8. Kentucky--History--Civil War, 1861-1865--Fiction.] I. Title.
  PZ7.H256272Gac 2008
  [Fic]--dc22
                                        2007042091

To the brave soldiers of the
Fifth United States Colored Cavalry
—A. H.

LIST OF CHARACTERS

Gabriel Alexander—thirteen-year-old groom and jockey who becomes a stable boy at Camp Nelson; a former slave of Mister Giles

Lucy Alexander—Gabriel's mother, a washerwoman at Camp Nelson

Jase and **Short Bit**—young grooms at Woodville Farm

Annabelle—thirteen-year-old former house slave and friend of Gabriel's

Mister Winston Giles—owner of Woodville Farm

Jackson—Gabriel's older friend and a jockey from Saratoga; returns to work for Mister Giles as a trainer

SOLDIERS AND OFFICERS OF COMPANY B OF THE FIFTH UNITED STATES COLORED CAVALRY (IN ORDER OF RANK):

Captain Henry Waite—commander of the Company B cavalry from Camp Nelson

Lieutenant Rhodes—commander of the 2nd Platoon

Sergeant Isaac Alexander—Gabriel's father, a trainer at Woodville Farm who enlisted in the Union army and is now stationed at Camp Nelson as commander of the 1st Squad

Corporal George Vaughn

Private Joseph Black

Private George Lewis

Private Andrew Crutcher

CAVALRY TERMS

squad—a group of soldiers made up of eight to twenty-four men; Sergeant Alexander, Gabriel's father, is commander of the 1st Squad.

platoon—a group of soldiers made up of two squads, with sixteen to fifty men; Lieutenant Rhodes is commander of the 1st Platoon.

company—a group of soldiers formed by two platoons, with sixty to a hundred men; Captain Henry Waite is commander of Company B.

regiment—a group of soldiers made up of companies, with 600 to 2,000 men. The Fifth United States Colored Cavalry was a regiment of about 600 black men hastily organized at Camp Nelson. It was commanded by Colonel James Wade, with assistance from Colonel James Brisbin. Historical records indicate that there were eleven companies in this regiment.

brigade—a group of soldiers made up of regiments, with the number of men dependent on the number of regiments. The 4th Brigade was made up of the Fifth, 11th Michigan, and 12th Ohio regiments; Colonel Ratliff of the 12th Ohio was commander of the 4th Brigade.

division—a group of soldiers made up of brigades. At the battle of Saltville, Major General Stephen Burbridge was commander of the Union division.

CHAPTER ONE

Keep your hands soft, Jase. Hard hands hurt a horse's mouth," I tell the young slave perched in the racing saddle. I'm leading Blind Patterson around Woodville Farm's grassy racing track. Jase is hunched over the Thoroughbred's neck, practicing being a jockey. "Don't use the reins for balance or pain. Use them to talk to your horse."

Jase bobs his head. Sweat beads on his brow.

"Now close your eyes," I go on in a hushed voice. "Feel Patterson's mouth. Listen to what he's telling you."

Jase shuts his eyes as I lead Patterson down the hill past the icehouse. "He sayin' he wants to gallop," Jase whispers. He pumps his arms as if they're flying toward the finish wire. The stallion stumbles, and Jase falls onto the horse's neck. He grabs mane and rights himself. "Not so fast, Gabriel," he scolds, though Patterson is walking as slow as an old nag. "This ain't a real race."

Chuckling erupts behind me. Jase shoots an angry look down at Short Bit, who's dogging my heels. Three weeks ago, when Mister Giles and me came home to Woodville Farm from Saratoga Springs, we brought Short Bit along as Aristo's groom. Since the first day Jase and Short Bit met, the boys ain't been apart. Except for their skin color—one white, one black—they're as close as the twin calves born here on the farm last spring.

"Why you chucklin' like a fool, Short Bit?" Jase asks. "Think you can ride dis horse better'n me?"

Short Bit nods eagerly.

I've been training the two of them since I came home. Both are small. Both love horses. Both will make fine jockeys. And Woodville Farm will need two fine riders someday soon if I leave.

If I leave. My stomach churns like I've been eating sour apples. I ain't told no one my thoughts on leaving Woodville Farm. Ain't told Mister Giles, Cato, Jase, or Annabelle that I'm thinking of going to Camp Nelson to be with Ma and Pa. Everyone knows I miss my folks with a fierce longing. But they also know how much I love horses and jockeying. Winning the Saratoga Chase on Aristo was like a week of Christmas. And since I've been home, I've won two more races on the colt.

Folks around here won't understand. "How can you leave the glory of winning," they'll ask me, "for a dirt-floor tent in an army camp?"

I'm too muddled to know the answer myself. But there's something else besides Ma and Pa tugging me toward Camp Nelson. The war between Confederate and Yankee has been going on for three long years. This past summer,

Kentucky slaves rushed to Camp Nelson to enlist in the Union army. Ma and Pa say I'm too young to be a soldier. And maybe at thirteen I ain't quite a man. But that don't mean I can't fight for freedom my own way.

Pa's a corporal under Captain Waite, the commander helping to organize a colored cavalry at Camp Nelson. Might be they won't let me wield a rifle against the Rebels, but I know I could help train those cavalry horses.

"Short Bit say it's his turn," Jase gasps from atop Blind Patterson.

I glance over my shoulder at Short Bit. The boy's cheeks have grown a lot plumper from Cook Nancy's biscuits and pies. Now his face is colored red by the sun, not by a bully's fists. And the wary look in his eyes is gone.

"You ready, Short Bit?" I ask.

Jase flops heavily back onto the saddle seat. "Says he is."

"I didn't hear Short Bit say nothin'."

Jase humphs. "*I* hear Short Bit clear as de dinner bell. He says, 'git dat black boy off dat horse so *I* can ride'." Kicking his bare feet from the stirrup irons, Jase slides to the ground.

It's the first of September, and the summer sun still blazes from the sky. Beyond the grassy track, I see a gang of field slaves plowing and planting. September means wheat and rye. Like all slaves, they work year-round, with one day off each week for the Sabbath. I still work six days even though I'm not a slave anymore. But now I don't have to call Mister Giles "master." I get paid for training and jock-eying, and I could walk to town without slave catchers coming after me.

Seems a crime so many coloreds are still someone's property.

Jase is struggling to boost Short Bit into the saddle. "Gabriel, give me a hand," he calls.

I blink, realizing I ain't paying attention. Racing and training horses take your whole mind, and right now, mine keeps scattering toward Ma, Pa, and the soldiers at Camp Nelson. That's reason enough to leave the farm.

Together, Jase and me toss Short Bit into the saddle. Slipping his bare feet into the irons, he gathers up the reins. The boy's beaming like a full moon.

I met Short Bit up in New York at the Saratoga Association Race Track, which is a long train ride from Woodville. An orphan, he'd lived most of his life in the barn with the Thoroughbreds, so he almost acts half-horse. But he'd always been a groom, not a rider.

"You ready, Short Bit?" I ask. For such a mite of a boy, he sits tall in the saddle, his fingers light on the reins. Crouching in the jockey position, he nods and squeezes his heels into Patterson's sides. Short Bit don't talk much, but the horses know what he's saying. Patterson strides right out, dragging me with him.

As Pa would say, *The boy's got the gift.*

We hop over the stream at the end of the grassy hill and turn toward the barns. Patterson breaks into a trot. Grinning, Short Bit moves in rhythm with the stallion's gait.

Jase is walking ahead, half hidden by tall grass, when suddenly he flies back toward us, his skinny legs pumping. "Miss Annabelle's comin'!" he shouts.

Short Bit's blue eyes bug from his head. I halt Patterson, and Jase darts behind me. I have no idea why the sight of Annabelle has turned my bold jockeys into field mice.

"There you shirkers are!" Annabelle hollers from the top of the hill. Her fists are planted on her hips. Her bonnet is askew as if she'd slapped it on her head in a big hurry. "I should've known it was you, Gabriel Alexander, making these scholars late for their lessons!"

Annabelle's thirteen, like me, but she grew up spoiled in the Main House. Before Mistress Jane died, she gave Annabelle her freedom, only Annabelle didn't know what to do with it. Since she was always bragging on her reading and writing, I told her she should teach the slaves. I wonder if I should've just kept my mouth shut since she's taking her schooling mighty seriously.

Annabelle, still dressed in mourning for Mistress Jane, strides down the hill, her long skirts flying. The black witch sight of her makes even *my* skin prickle.

With a squeak, Short Bit jumps off Patterson.

Annabelle steps in front of us, her dark eyes snapping. "It's an hour after noon. You two are late for arithmetic." She grabs each boy by an ear and starts dragging them up the hill. Howling, they stumble after her.

"Annabelle," I call after her, "don't you know nothin' about teaching?"

She stops, keeping her fingers firmly pinched on those ears.

"Horses taught with kindness learn much faster than those taught with the whip," I point out.

5

"Oh! Thank you for your pretty sermon, Gabriel. And when I start teaching horses to read and write, I'll be sure to heed your words," she says tartly.

Jase and Short Bit giggle. Annabelle lets go of their ears and herds them toward the Main House with shooing motions. Laughing, they dodge her flapping hands, and I gather their fear of Annabelle is more mock than real.

"Come on, Patterson. Racin' is over." I lead him up the hill, through the gate, and down the lane past the horse pastures. Aristo's in the first paddock. Tossing his head, the colt prances over, his reddish gold coat rippling like sun-kissed water. He pins his ears and nips at Patterson, who ignores his gnashing teeth.

I scratch the colt's neck. Aristo wheels and gallops across the pasture, stirring up the colts and fillies in the other fields. As I watch them gambol, my stomach roils again. If I leave Woodville Farm, who will look out for the horses? *Who will jockey Aristo?*

Slipping my hand in my pocket, I pull out the tattered article cut from the *Daily Saratogian.* Annabelle's read it to me twenty times so I know the words by heart:

…gallantly jockey Alexander rode the game and speedy Aristo, who held his own down the stretch. In spite of the determined rush of Faraway, the Kentucky bred dashed under the wire to win one of the fastest-run races ever seen on this track.

Ever since I started riding, I dreamed of seeing my name in a newspaper. Now there it is: *jockey Alexander.* How can I give up the triumph I fought so hard for?

Folding the article, I tuck it in my pocket and cluck to

Patterson. We amble over to the red-brick training barn. Mister Giles is walking toward us from the Main House. He's wearing a top hat like he's off to the city. A surrey awaits him at the roundabout in front of the carriage horse barn. When he spies me and Patterson, he calls out a hearty good day.

"Good day, Mister Giles," I call back.

"You're just the chap I need to talk to," he says in his British accent. Mister Giles came to Kentucky from England, which is even farther from here than New York. Before my folks left for Camp Nelson, Pa worked as his trainer and Ma as his house servant. I was born at Woodville Farm, so it has always been my home.

I halt Patterson in the doorway of the barn. Mister Giles has a good eye for horseflesh and owns some of the fastest Thoroughbreds in Kentucky. Lifting the saddle flap, I unbuckle Patterson's girth.

"I have grand news, Gabriel." Mister Giles waves his cane at me as he approaches. "I'm off to pick up a new trainer at the Midway station. He's arriving from New York."

I stiffen. Newcastle, the last trainer Mister Giles brought from the North, used a whip and a curse to train the horses.

"The man comes highly recommended. *Highly,*" Mister Giles repeats, sounding as gleeful as a child in a sweet shop.

"That's fine, sir." I slide the saddle from Patterson's back.

"I had to offer him a handsome wage to leave the North. The man likes his fancy duds and his pretty ladies." Mister Giles gives me a sly wink. "I also had to promise him

7

a percent of the purse money *and* a home of his own made of brick, not wood, with windows of glass. The man knows what he wants, but he'll be worth every pane."

My brows rise as Mister Giles's words sink in. There's only one fancy-dressing ladies' man I know who could come close to Pa: *Jackson!* But it can't be Jackson. When I left my friend in New York, he was riding for Doctor Crown, and well satisfied with his new life.

Mister Giles raps the tip of his cane on the ground. "This man won't replace your pa, Gabriel, but he'll come mighty close."

"Is it Jackson, sir?" I dare ask.

"It is indeed," says Mr. Giles, holding back a smile. "I told him the war would soon be over and all coloreds would be free. Then every black horseman will head north for the racetracks. By then, Jackson will be well established here and training champions." A grin lifts his mustache. "Think of it, Gabriel. With him training and you riding, we can travel the States, racing and winning at every track."

Goosebumps trot up my arms. He's right. Jackson, me, and Mister Giles's Thoroughbreds would be *unbeatable.*

Instantly my muddled thoughts grow clear. "Sir, it is a tempting offer, but I'll have to say no thank you."

Mister Giles starts in surprise. "You have bigger plans?"

"I'm going to Camp Nelson to be with Ma and Pa," I explain. "I didn't want to leave the horses in the care of a no-account trainer like Newcastle. But now that I know Jackson's taking Pa's place, my mind's made up to go."

Mister Giles studies my face. "I'd hate to lose you,

Gabriel," he says. "You're a natural with horses. You were born to ride."

"I do love the horses," I admit, "but my time for riding will have to wait. Now my place is with Ma and Pa."

Mister Giles places one gloved hand on my shoulder. "I was afraid of this. Your family bond is strong. And I've seen a faraway look in your eyes for a few days now. I was hoping Jackson's return to Woodville might entice you to stay."

"It is good news, sir, but Ma's getting big with child and Pa's training cavalry horses. I need to be with them."

Mister Giles shakes his head in dismay. "You are a gifted jockey, Gabriel, and you'll be hard to replace."

"Short Bit's turning into a right smart rider," I tell him. "Jackson can jockey until he gets too heavy from Cook Nancy's cobblers, and by then Short Bit will be ready to take his place."

"You see potential in Short Bit, eh?" Mister Giles asks.

"Yes sir."

"And the glory of winning races won't make you reconsider your decision to leave?"

"No sir." I throw back my shoulders a bit. "The glory of helping to win this war will have to be enough."

"Patriotic thoughts, Gabriel." Mister Giles places both hands on the top of his cane. "Let's hope the realities of war won't tarnish them. If you're set on this course, I'll telegraph ahead to Captain Waite."

"Thank you, sir." Now that I've told Mister Giles of my decision to join Ma and Pa, excitement flares in my chest.

I picture myself drilling with Pa's squad. Soon I'll learn how to march double-quick, fire a rifle, and salute the officers.

Tomorrow, I'll pack my belongings and say farewell to my friends—and to my beloved horses. Then, with my head held high, I'll stride down the Frankfort Pike on the start of my new journey.

CHAPTER TWO

I soon find that *thinking* farewell is a heap easier than *saying* farewell. It's morning and Jackson and me are in the supply room in the barn. Last night was the first time I'd seen my friend since New York, and here I am, aiming to leave him.

"One reason I came back to Woodville was to work with you, Gabriel," Jackson says, a piece of straw poking from between his lips. "Why don't you stay a few weeks? We can win some races—*and* some purse money—afore you leave."

I shake my head. I've already resolved that no words or deeds will sway me from my decision. "I've won my share," I tell him. "My mind's on soldiering now."

Jackson heaves a sigh. I know his thoughts on this war because we've had this conversation already. Jackson believes fighting and dying for freedom is foolish. He says coloreds will be free when they have a skill that earns them money. For Jackson, that's training and jockeying horses.

He takes the straw from his mouth and points the stalk

at me. "You are one mule-headed boy. Ain't nothin' going to change your thoughts on soldiering, am I right?"

I nod.

"Well, then, I suppose you'd best join your folks." Grinning, Jackson raises his fists and takes up a boxing stance. For a moment we spar the air, and then he hugs me hard and quick. Before I can open my mouth to tell him *I'll be back someday,* he's out the supply room door.

Now it's my turn to heave a sigh. I've already bid farewell to Jase, Short Bit, Tandy, and the other stable workers. And I've said goodbye to Cook Nancy, who packed me a basket of vittles, and to Mister Giles, who helped me get permission to enter Camp Nelson. But saying goodbye to all of them together ain't nearly so hard as saying goodbye to Annabelle.

I find her in the parlor of the Main House. She's sashaying around the room, whooshing a duster in the air. She starts chattering about yesterday's lessons with Jase and Short Bit. "Short Bit can recite the alphabet and Jase can write his name. I know you're learning your numbers on account of all the purse money you're winning, but you need to join our lessons, Gabriel. If you don't, you'll be the only stable boy who can't read."

"I'd like to learn to read, Annabelle," I say, my tone wooden.

"And do you know that Cook Nancy's written a letter to your ma already?" Annabelle asks. I know by the way she's attacking the chair rungs with those feathers that she don't expect an answer. "And Mister Giles has entrusted me with his correspondence. He's appointed me his secretary."

"That's a powerful title."

"I do believe you're right, Gabriel," she agrees. "Secretary sounds so much grander than slave." She spits out *slave* like it's a cuss word, then patters on. "Mister Giles says this war will soon be over and every slave will be free. Then we'll all be paid wages, like you and Jackson. He says that those who can read and write will be highly valued."

"Maybe I can join Ma for reading and writing lessons at Camp Nelson. Reverend Fee has a school there."

"Pish posh." Annabelle's back is to me as she swipes the feathers along a picture frame. "Why, I can teach better than some wattle-necked old…" Her voice trails off. Tilting her head, she looks at me over her shoulder. A frown creases her brow. "What did you say?"

I gulp. Annabelle's piercing eyes have a way of tying my tongue. "I-I said I'll soon be leaving for Camp Nelson."

"For a visit?"

I shake my head.

"For*ever?*" The feather duster drops from Annabelle's fingers and the handle clatters on the wooden floor. Her lower lip trembles.

Holding my breath, I nod. Then I clench my hands behind me, girding myself for her sharp cry and flood of tears. Instead she ducks her head and rushes from the room, soundless except for the rustling of her skirts.

I gaze after her as she flees like an apparition up the winding stairs.

"Annabelle!" I call, but her name sticks in my throat.

You are a treed possum, I think, cursing myself. Why is it so hard to tell her that I'll miss her? Folks say I have a magic touch with horses, but those charms sure fail me with Annabelle.

Hurrying from the parlor into the entrance hall, I look up the stairs. Silence floats from the second floor. I strain my ears, and when I don't hear the scuffle of returning shoes, sorrow fills me. As soon as I get to Camp Nelson, I'll learn my letters so I can pen Annabelle a proper goodbye.

Bong...bong... The clock in the parlor strikes seven times. It's time to go. I can't tarry any longer.

My eyes cut to the carved panels on the front door. Slaves are forbidden to use the main entrance unless they're serving the master, but I'm a slave no more. This may be the last time I leave this house.

I grasp the shiny brass knob, heave open the door, and walk boldly onto the veranda.

Morning sun streams from the east. At the bottom of the stairs, Old Uncle kneels in the rose garden. He's picking beetles off the leaves and pinching them between his finger and thumb. He glances up. I expect a surprised look when he sees a black boy standing on the portico, but his brown, wrinkled face is a mask.

"I hear you's leavin'," Old Uncle says, his attention back on the beetles, which have chewed lacey holes in the leaves.

I thump down the steps. "Yes sir. I came to say goodbye."

"Followin' your ma and pa to Camp Nelson?"

"Yes sir."

He grunts, as if satisfied. "A family should be together."

I hear a crunch as he snaps another beetle. "Take care, Old Uncle."

"And you, Gabriel Alexander."

I jog down the walkway and underneath the arched trellis. I need to retrieve my packed belongings from the barn—and say goodbye to the horses.

My innards clench. I've put it off as long as I can.

I drag my feet the whole way to the training barn, which is as silent as the Main House. All the workers are at the carriage barn, meeting to discuss contracts and wages. Seems Mister Giles forgot to mention Jackson's most important demand—that grooms and stable hands at Woodville Farm be treated as free men.

Since the flies are biting, the colts and fillies have been brought in for the day. I make my way slowly down the aisle, stopping at each stall. Savannah, Captain, Daphne, Arrow, Blind Patterson, Tenpenny, Sympathy, and at the end of the row, Aristo. Heads dip as they munch sweet hay. I breathe their scent one last time, admiring the sheen of their coats, the ripple of their muscles, the light in their eyes. I don't want to forget them—ever.

Leaning over Aristo's door, I glide my fingers down his silky neck. He nuzzles my cheek and chews close to my ear.

"'Risto," I whisper. "You are the finest colt in the States, and I'm honored to have been your jockey."

As long as I can remember, these have been *my* horses. How can I tell them goodbye?

I can't.

Tears threaten, reminding me I ain't a man yet. I dash

down the aisle to the supply room, snatch up my basket and my blanket-wrapped bundle, and bolt from the barn.

My bare feet pound the lane as I race past the Main House, the basket thumping my leg. I can't hold back the tears and they roll down my cheeks, plopping from my chin like raindrops. I run past the armed guard at the end of the lane. Then, turning east on the Frankfort Pike, I fly across the bridge. I run until a stitch splits my ribs, and I finally double over, gasping. When I catch my breath and steal a glance over my shoulder, Woodville Farm is long behind me.

★ ★ ★

The sun is high overhead so I know I've been walking a good four hours. I'm wrapped in misery and loneliness, and my stomach grumbles. Cook Nancy's vittles disappeared by the third mile, and the basket's as empty as my insides—and my heart.

I've left the only place I've ever called home, and the only folks I've ever called friends.

A stick snaps in the brush, and I jump like a startled rabbit. Part of me expects to see Keats and Butler, those Rebel no-goods who stole Captain Conrad and knocked me senseless. Another part of me worries that One Arm Dan Parmer and his band might be back in Kentucky.

Even though I've traveled to Camp Nelson before, I've always had company. This time I'm one skinny, scared boy on my own.

The rattle of wheels makes me whirl in my tracks. A

pony's muzzle, followed by a pair of fuzzy ears, pokes through a cloud of dust kicked up by a peddler's wagon. I spring to the roadside, clutching my bundle. The pony has a hitch in its walk, so it moseys by me, and I'm in no danger of being crushed by its hooves.

A gnarled white man sits on the wagon seat. Behind him, keys dangle and sway from rows of hooks. The man peers at me with one eye; the other is an empty socket. A dirty rag is wrapped around his forehead. Too late, he tugs it down, angling it over the puckered flesh.

I stare back, never having seen a man with one eye.

"Whoa, Betsy," the man says. The pony halts with a wheezy sigh. Cocking his head like a robin at a wormhole, the man studies me. Golden letters and curlicues decorate the wooden sides of his wagon, which looks like a box on wheels.

"Good day, sir," I say hesitantly.

"*Good* day? I'd say it's a *bad* day," he barks. "At least bad for you, colored boy. Why, you're a sorrier sight than me. And I'm 'bout as sorry as they come."

"Yes sir."

"*Yes* sir? Are you agreeing that I'm 'bout as sorry as they come?"

"No sir!"

"You should say, 'No sir, I ain't sorry at all. I've got my youth and my two feet and my future ahead of me.'"

"Uh-h-h," I stammer, not daring to reply nay or yea.

He cackles. "Don't mind me. I'm daft. Least that's what the Rebels said afore they stole my wares."

"Rebels! Was it One Arm Dan Parmer?"

Rubbing his chin, gray with dirt and stubble, he thinks a moment. "Captain in charge did have one arm. Might be why he took pity and didn't shoot me—'cause we had that number in common."

I shudder. "Is One Arm and his band of guerrillas headed this way?"

"Nah. Those Rebels know better than to show their scoundrel selves this close to Lexington. Where are you headed, black boy?"

"Camp Nelson."

"I'm headed into the city to report those thieves and restock my wagon. But I don't mind traveling the outskirts a ways if you'd like me to drop you at the Danville Pike."

"I'd be obliged." I nod up at the keys. "Luckily they didn't steal those."

"Pah! They don't want keys, since they have no doors. They stole everything else though: eyeglasses, tonics, combs, even a dozen cans of peaches."

My mouth waters at the mention of peaches.

"But they didn't find my cash." He winks his one eye. "Climb aboard, youngun. Betsy and I could use the company. Unlike most folks around these parts, we ain't choosy about a traveler's skin color."

I toss my bundle and basket into the back of his wagon, which is empty except for a pile of moth-eaten blankets, a stained ticking-striped pillow, and a feed bucket filled with moldy corn. I guess even the Rebels weren't that desperate.

Using the wheel spokes like rungs, I clamber into the

wagon. He holds out one grubby hand. "Name's Pie." His clothes smell as if they ain't been washed in his lifetime.

We shake and I say, "Pleased to meet you, Mister Pie. My name's Gabriel Alexander."

He clucks to Betsy, who gimps off. I sway in the wagon seat, glad for the companionship no matter how odorous.

"Name's Pie 'cause I used to sell pies," he explains, even though I didn't ask. "Then it became One-Eye Pie, and now it's back to jest Pie. Lost my eye in the war. A redcoat shot it clean through with a lead ball."

"A redcoat?" I know about redcoats on account of Mister Giles being British. "They ain't fighting in this war."

"*This* war!" He harrumphs in disgust. "I'm talking about the War of 1812 when we were fighting those blackhearts the British, not shooting at our neighbors."

I goggle at him. If Pie was fighting in 1812, then he's older than Old Uncle.

"I was 'bout your size when I enlisted. Lied and told 'em I was sixteen." Pie launches into a tale of joining up with the U.S. Army. As he jabbers on, I gradually sag against the back of the wagon, half-asleep.

Suddenly Pie's voice rises, waking me from my stupor. "The firing was deafening!" he shouts. "All around me, soldiers toppled to the ground until I was tripping over bloody arms and limbs. Then I found myself face to face with a redcoat. A boy 'bout my age. We gaped at each other, then raised our muskets." Dropping the reins onto his lap, Pie holds an imaginary rifle against his shoulder and aims. "I pressed the trigger, but nothing happened." He grunts.

"In the confusion, I'd forgotten to reload. My first skirmish and I lose my eye to a British boy's bayonet!"

Didn't he say a mile back that his eye had been shot out with a lead ball? "My pa's at Camp Nelson," I say, hoping to get him onto another subject.

"Your pa's a colored soldier?"

I nod proudly. "A corporal in the Union army. He's helping Colonel Waite organize a colored cavalry. I aim to join him and train cavalry horses so we can beat the Confederates."

Pie harrumphs. "If you ask me, this is a dang-burned foolish war."

"It ain't foolish at all," I protest. "We're fightin' the Rebels 'cause they don't want slaves to be free."

He points to the rag around his head. "Just pray no Rebel takes your eye. Did I mention how a shard from a cannonball knocked mine clean out? Whoa, Betsy." Stopping the pony, Pie gestures to the right, and I recognize the Lexington and Danville Turnpike. "This is your jumping-off point, youngun."

I hop from the seat and yank my bundle from the wagon bed, leaving the empty basket as meager payment. "Much obliged for the ride, Mister Pie—and for your company." Tossing my bundle over my shoulder, I head south on the Pike wishing I'd had more time to set Mister Pie straight about this war.

I keep up a brisk pace. The road is empty. Not a sign of life except a few crows picking in the cornfield beyond a stone fence. As I walk, I sing "Sweet Lorena" to chase away the silence. But the song is Savannah's favorite, and it reminds me how much I miss those horses. I switch to a hymn instead. My singing startles the crows and they flap toward the sky. I hope the black birds circling over my head ain't bad omens. I'm uneasy enough about this journey.

My innards grumble and I eye the drying ears of corn. It's field corn for livestock, I know, but it's long after noon mealtime and right now my stomach ain't particular.

I glance up and down the road, making sure I'm alone. Reaching far over the stone fence, I grab an ear and twist it from the stalk. Then I hunker behind some brush where I can't be seen from the road.

I strip away the husk. The orange-yellow kernels are as hard as acorns in the shell, but I chew a few to a pulp, swallow, and start on a second row. Soon the rumbling quiets in my insides. I'm wishing for a plate of Cook Nancy's cornbread when I hear rustling in the stalks behind me.

My jaw stops in mid-chew.

Dry leaves crackle. A stalk snaps. *Someone's stomping through that corn.*

I stare guiltily at the half-eaten cob in my hand. Thieves have been hanged for less!

CHAPTER THREE

Quickly, I toss the ear of corn over my shoulder. Someone hollers, "Ow!" It's a holler I've heard many times before. I rise from my hiding place and peer over the stone fence. Between the leaves I spy striped taffeta.

A gloved hand pushes a stalk aside and a girl steps from the rows. Her straw hat is askew and corn mold dusts her chin.

"Annabelle? Is that you?"

"It is, Gabriel," she replies. Her chin is tipped up defiantly despite the sweat trickling down her cheeks and the hair straggling from under her crooked hat brim.

My mouth falls slack. I'd expected to see a riled-up farmer or a vagrant, not a girl in a taffeta skirt. "What are you doing here in a cornfield, dressed for tea?"

"Hush your teasing and help me over this fence."

Grasping Annabelle's hand, I tug her to the top of the stone wall. She's wearing layers of fabric over petticoats, and the whole affair billows in my face, threatening to smother me. I'm astounded she isn't wrestling a parasol through the corn, too. She teeters a moment atop the fence, then jumps to the ground, falling against my chest. Heat creeps up my neck.

We spring apart, and I notice her cheeks are as flushed as mine. "Thank you," she says breathlessly as she rights her straw hat. Black-eyed Susans poke from the hatband, as if she'd had time to dally by the wayside and pick them.

"I'd be much obliged if you'd retrieve my belongings." She waves toward the cornfield, and I see a basket, a valise, and a *parasol* on the ground between two rows.

I hesitate. I want to be gallant, but I know how corn leaves tear at your skin. Since Annabelle is garbed from head to toe, she escaped most of their slashes. My arms and feet are bare.

"The basket's packed with honey, bread, and rabbit pie," Annabelle says sweetly.

In two shakes I'm over that fence and back, not minding the scratches on my arms. I hand her the parasol and hustle down the pike to a shady tree, carrying the basket and valise. Annabelle takes her time catching up with me. She removes a small quilt from the basket and spreads it out like we're having a noon picnic. She sinks onto the quilt and arranges her skirts in a ladylike manner. After tugging the purse strings from her wrist and carefully pulling off her gloves, she opens the basket and sets out the food.

I kneel next to her, drooling at the sight of Cook Nancy's bread and pie, their crusts flaky and golden. Annabelle's quiet as she rips off a chunk of bread and dribbles honey on it. I'm bursting to find out why she was hiding in a cornfield beside the road to Camp Nelson, but I gather she'll tell her tale when we're both fed.

She hands the bread to me. "Ladies first," I say despite my hunger.

"Please take it," she says softly. I hear a catch in her voice, as if she's holding back tears.

Leaning on one elbow, I gobble the bread, my gaze on Annabelle. She keeps her head lowered as she honeys some bread for herself. She takes tiny bites while I wolf down a second slice.

Finally Annabelle dabs her lips with a linen napkin. "I suppose you're wondering why I'm here. And rest assured it is *not* because I missed you."

I raise my eyes to the heavens. "Thank the Lord."

She looks up sharply. When she sees I'm grinning, she hurls a wooden spoon, which I dodge. "You should thank the Lord I came along, Gabriel, since it appears you were near to starving." She serves me rabbit pie on a tin plate. "Go on. I ate a roasted potato while I walked."

I pick up the wooden spoon and dig in. "If you didn't follow me, how'd you know the way?" I ask between chews.

Her nostrils flare. "I can read road signs and maps, of course."

"Then how'd you get lost and end up in a cornfield?"

"I wasn't *lost.*" Even when Annabelle frowns, she's rose-garden pretty. "I was being careful. At the crossroads, I spied two white men approaching from the north. They were still off quite a distance, but I felt uneasy. A girl traveling alone can't be too cautious." She trails her fingers down her skirt. "I wore one of Mistress Jane's outfits, hoping that dressing like a lady would keep menfolk respectful. As the men drew nearer, though, I grew faint of heart and ducked into the cornfield."

I eat slowly, entranced by her story.

Her voice quivers. "I kept one eye on the stone fence as I headed south, hoping I wouldn't lose my way. But those jagged cornstalks dragged at me like claws, and the roots grabbed at my feet. My limbs and my courage were about to give out when I heard you singing 'Sweet Lorena'." She presses one palm against her bodice. "Oh, Gabriel, you have no idea how glad I was to see you."

I redden, flustered by her declaration. "How'd you catch up to me so fast?"

"Fast? That peddler's cart you were traveling in was moving as slow as a turtle in a strawberry patch."

"Some would say you were a dad-burned fool to set out alone, but I think you were brave. That still don't explain why you followed me."

"Who says I followed you?" Annabelle busies herself with tidying up. "I'm traveling to Camp Nelson as well."

"To visit?"

"To stay."

"But I thought you were happy being Mister Giles's secretary."

"I was, but I realized as long as I live in that house, I'll never feel free."

I shake my head. "Annabelle, it took me more than a fortnight to decide to leave. You made up your mind in a finger snap."

"So?" she huffs.

I know by her tone that it ain't no use arguing my point. Instead, I stuff the last of the rabbit pie into my mouth and belch heartily.

"Gabriel! Such un-gentlemanly behavior. Excuse yourself."

"I won't. And stop bein' bossy on me, Annabelle. Just 'cause you're *dressed* like Mistress don't mean you *are* one." I boldly reach out and flick a bread crumb off her bottom lip.

She slaps my hand away. "Of all the impertinence!"

"Don't know what that word means and don't care." I jump to my feet. "But if we're traveling together, you need to stop being so high and mighty. 'Sides, at Camp Nelson, all coloreds are equal."

"We'll see about that." She starts packing bread and pie back in the basket, her mouth pressed in a line.

"What's that mean, 'we'll see'?"

She pats the purse in her lap. "It means *I* have a letter from Mister Giles addressed to Brigadier General Speed S. Fry respectfully recommending that the Union army employ me as a secretary."

I stare at her in disbelief. Mister Giles would never give her such a letter, let alone allow her to travel on her own.

"You doubt me?" she challenges.

26

"I do." Bending forward, I snatch up her purse and loosen the strings. Ladylike no longer, she squeals like a poked pig and lunges for it, knocking me flat.

I scrabble backwards, pull the letter from the purse, and unfold it. I may not be as smart as Annabelle when it comes to reading, but I've seen Mister Giles's writing enough to recognize it ain't his signature at the bottom. "You forged this letter *and* his name. That's a federal offense."

"Only if the authorities catch me." Plucking the letter from my grasp, she tucks it into her purse and draws tight the strings. "Besides, as Mister Giles's *secretary* I've been writing and signing all his letters."

"Did you forge your free papers, too?" I ask.

She shakes her head as she slips her gloves back on. "I went to the courthouse with Mister Giles for that." Rising primly, she ruffles her skirt and adjusts her hat. "Now we'd best be on our way," she says, and pops opens the parasol.

Annabelle sashays off, basket in one hand, frilled parasol in the other. Dumbfounded, I stare after her. I can't fathom if she's courageous or downright foolhardy. Annabelle knows nothing of Camp Nelson, but from my prior visits I can say for sure that the place ain't for a lady, especially one with black skin. Ma's got Pa, and even she is living in a tent and washing soldiers' underdrawers.

With a shake of my head, I stand and pick up Annabelle's valise and my bundle. Raucous cawing comes from overhead. Four crows have gathered in the tree boughs. They peer down at me, silhouetted against the sky like haunts.

I've heard tell that crows are harbingers of death.

I start after Annabelle, my mind awhirl. What awaits her at the end of this journey, I don't know, but I say a silent prayer that she won't regret her decision.

As we travel south, the bright sun chases away the thoughts of haunts. Having Annabelle along slows our traveling. Every mile she stops to pry pebbles from her shoes and slap dust off her skirt. Still she joins in when I sing "Camptown Races" and listens eagerly to my stories of Saratoga. I'm glad for her company.

The sun is dropping behind the trees when we finally come upon the first of the many refugee camps that dot the roadsides before the entryway into Camp Nelson. Annabelle has never heard of refugees, so I explain that these are slave women and families who followed their husbands or fathers to Camp Nelson, or who were thrown off their masters' farms. I warn Annabelle about the stick-skinny black children, and when a horde of them clusters around us, grabbing at Annabelle's skirts, purse, and valise, she tries not to shrink against me.

I've learned some tricks from my other trips to the camp. Pulling pennies from my pocket, I toss them into the grass and weeds. The children scatter like chickens after corn, and we hurry past the shanties and makeshift tents. A bone-weary black lady stooped over an iron pot calls to me, "Boy, are you entering Camp Nelson?"

"Yes ma'am," I reply.

Dropping her wooden spoon, the woman hastens over.

She clasps her fingers around my arm and begs me to find her man, Private John Barrett. "Tell him baby Ellen has died of the fever," she says.

A dozen more women quickly gather round me and Annabelle. Their homespun dresses are threadbare, their cheeks are hollow, and there's desperation in their eyes as they implore us to take word to recruits, laborers, and soldiers inside the camp. Annabelle repeats names, trying to remember them. But I notice that the women direct their urgent messages at me and cast suspicious glances at Annabelle.

When we finally break away from them, Annabelle is breathing hard. She presses a handkerchief to her mouth as we hurry the last few yards toward the entrance.

"Gabriel," she whispers from behind the white lace hanky, "I've never seen such dirt and hunger and sadness. I tried to be polite and helpful, but no one would even grace me with a look!"

"Perhaps they've never seen a colored girl wearing taffeta and carrying a parasol," I say, my voice low, too. "Nor heard one who speaks like a white lady."

Halting in her tracks, Annabelle stares at me. "Am I so different?"

I curse my tongue. No matter what I reply, it will not suit Annabelle. To my relief I'm spared further questions by the approach of a guard in Union blue.

"State your business," he says, his young face grave beneath the brim of his forage cap.

I pull a telegraph from my bundle. "I'm here on orders from Captain Waite. I'm to work with the colored cavalry." I try to sound official, but my knees knock. Mister Giles personally telegraphed Captain Waite, who telegraphed this message in reply. The two became acquainted when Captain Waite's white company of soldiers helped saved Woodville Farm from One Arm and his raiders. But what if this picket doesn't let me in?

He passes the telegraph back to me. "You'll bunk in the tents of the colored cavalry," he snaps, "on the hill behind the colored barracks."

I exhale in relief.

Giving him a pert smile, Annabelle hands him her letter. "And I am here to meet with Brigadier General Speed S. Fry."

He skims the letter, then hands it back to her with a dismissive snort. "The brigadier general doesn't need a secretary."

"Oh, but I write letters in the finest hand," Annabelle explains.

"Except it's a *colored* hand," he says curtly. "Brigadier General Fry is plagued with Negro women sneaking in to camp. He sure ain't going to invite one in. Even a *lady*," he adds with a smirk, "who's wearing fancy clothes—likely stolen from her mistress." He jerks his thumb toward the refugee shanties. "Be on your way."

Annabelle opens her mouth to protest, only for once, she's speechless.

A commotion causes all three of us to look toward the

entrance. A cluster of black women, tied together with ropes around their waists, is being herded from the camp. Union soldiers flank them. When one woman stumbles, a soldier prods her with his rifle butt. "Quit stalling," he snarls. "Mister Wilkes will be here any minute to fetch you."

Just then, an open-bed wagon rattles down the pike from the direction of Lexington. A ruddy-faced man with a clipped beard and derby hat is driving the team, cracking a whip over the horses. I hear sobs from the women and one cries out, "Lord save us!"

The wagon thunders toward us. Grabbing Annabelle's elbow, I swing her out of the way. Her parasol slips from her grasp, and the wheels crush it flat.

"Whoa!" The man saws on the horses' bits with the reins until the animals halt in front of the soldiers and women.

"Gabriel, what's happening?" Annabelle asks.

I shush her with a finger in front of my mouth. The unfolding scene reminds me of the first time I visited Camp Nelson. That day, slaves were marching into camp as recruits, and masters were demanding that they be returned. There was a heap of confusion. If this turns into a ruckus, too, I aim to take advantage.

"Thank you, Lieutenant Sawyer, for securing my property," the man tells one of the soldiers. "They all belong to me. Load 'em up."

The soldiers roughly escort the bound group of women to the end of the wagon. "Get in!" Lieutenant Sawyer orders as he drops the hinged end gate. The soldiers begin lifting and shoving the women, who are still lashed together. They struggle mightily, and one cusses and kicks out. Immediately the others start screeching, and the sentinels at the entrance rush to help.

I nudge Annabelle. "Quick, follow me." Ducking, I run to the camp entrance, momentarily unguarded. Basket bobbling and skirts flying, Annabelle chases after me.

I make it through the gap in the fortifications without losing my bundle or the valise. Turning, I gesture to Annabelle to hurry. One hand holds her straw hat, and I can see the fear on her face.

I hear the crack of a whip outside the gates. It sounds like someone is thrashing a horse—or a human. A woman screams. My guts jump into my throat.

I shove my bundle under my arm and grab Annabelle's gloved hand, and together we race into Camp Nelson as if the Devil himself is after us.

CHAPTER FOUR

Hands linked, Annabelle and I pound past the White House, where the officers bunk. I'm bent on making straight for Ma's tent, but Annabelle stumbles. "Gabriel," she pants. "I...can't...run...any...farther."

I pull her behind a stack of timbers, and we stop to catch our breath.

"My heels have blisters, and oh, look at my dress!" Annabelle lifts her skirts a trace. The hems are muddy and torn. "How can I present myself to the brigadier general like this?" she wails.

She's so upset, I don't tell her that her hair's as wild as weeds, the black-eyed Susans are droopy, and *there ain't a chance in heaven she'll ever get a meeting with the brigadier general.*

A short distance away, three Negroes are splitting logs. They halt their ax swinging to stare at us. One winks at Annabelle, and another calls to me, "Boy, you sure caught yourself a purty gal. Better not let go of her unless you want me to take her."

I yank Annabelle back onto the road, cursing myself. I was right about this being no place for a lady, even Annabelle. When I met up with her by the cornfield, I should have sent her straight back to Woodville Farm, no matter how loudly she protested.

I search for a hiding place. By now, Annabelle and the valise are lead weights on my arms. If we keep running, we're going to attract suspicion. I'm not sure where the tents of the colored cavalry are located, but I do know where Ma is living. Her tent is a long way from here, and I don't believe Annabelle can make it without a rest.

A squad of soldiers marches down the road toward us. I slow to a walk. "Thank you," Annabelle puffs. "My corset's pinching and I was about to give out."

"Act like we belong here," I say under my breath. "Be quiet and pretend like we know where we're going."

Annabelle sees the soldiers, too. She straightens her crooked hat and smoothes her dusty skirts. Linking her free arm with mine, she tips her chin and we stride purposefully down the road. "I could pretend much easier if I had my parasol," Annabelle whispers. When the soldiers pass, she bobs her head politely and calls, "Good day, gentlemen."

They don't break formation as they march by, but it's only a matter of time until someone does stop to question us. "Just keep your mouth shut," I warn her. "There's a stable ahead. We can hide in a hay shed until dark and then find Ma's tent."

The stable yard is busy with soldiers grooming horses and putting them up for the night. Immediately I think of

Woodville Farm, and a pang hits me. Are Tandy, Jase, and Short Bit taking good care of Aristo and the other horses?

Nearby, blacksmiths tend the coal fires and shape horseshoes on anvils. Like thieves, Annabelle and I sneak behind the stable, the dusk masking us. I spot a three-sided straw shed tucked a ways from the road and drag her inside.

Annabelle sinks into the pile of straw. "This feels better than a feather mattress," she says. She takes off her hat and, using my bundle for a pillow, curls up in the hay. "Thanks for all you did, Gab'iel," she says, the words slurring in her weariness. "A lady could not have as't for a more gallan' escort..." Her lashes flutter, her breathing slows, and an instant later she's asleep.

I scatter straw over her skirts, then cover the basket and valise so no one will spot them. I try to stay awake—it won't be long before dark and we'll have to be on the move again. I also need to keep watch for stable hands bearing pitchforks. But my eyelids soon grow heavy. Even though straw dust tickles my nose and the blacksmiths' hammers clang in my ears, I burrow into the mound and drift off, too.

★ ★ ★

A calloused hand roughly shakes me. I've been dreaming about the fire in the barn at Saratoga, and I thrash awake. Golden light blinds me, and I cover my eyes with my fingers, shielding them from the flames. "Fire!" I holler. "Save the—"

A palm slaps over my mouth. "Hush, boy, 'fore you wakes de dead."

My eyes gape. An old black man is staring down at me. A lantern in his hand is shining in my face. "Dere ain't no fire," he says. "So hush."

I nod to show him I understand, and he removes his hand. He smells like horse manure, so I gather he's a stable worker.

"Soldiers on night watch patrol 'round dese barns," he says in a low voice. "You best skedaddle 'fore dey catch you and toss you from de camp."

"Thanks for the warning." I glance behind me, hoping Annabelle knows not to stir from her hiding place. I glimpse the toe of her shoe poking from the straw, and pray the old man doesn't notice. I jump up to block his view. "What's the quickest way to the washerwomen's tents?" I ask. "My ma lives there. She's doing laundry for the colored cavalry."

"Go down de pike past Camp Nelson House. Dere's a lane to de east. De colored cavalry are bunking in tents on de hillside. Stay off de road—guards be patrollin'."

"How far once we turn onto the lane?"

"If you fall into Hickman Creek, you've gone too far." Chuckling, he raises the lantern and heads off.

I tap Annabelle's shoe. "Wake up," I whisper. "We need to go." I uncover the valise and basket and brush them off. By the time I'm finished, Annabelle's standing and shaking the hay off her dress. It's too dark to see her face, but she's hastily tying her hat. I gather she realizes the urgency.

Voices drift from the front of the stable, and my blood quickens. I toss the bundle over my shoulder and pick up the valise. Annabelle takes my hand in hers, and we steal silently into the shadows.

To stay on course, we follow the direction of the pike, but instead of marching like soldiers, we scurry like mice between buildings, woodpiles, and sheds. Finally we reach the dirt lane and head east. I hope the old man's right. When Ma, Jase, and me came to Camp Nelson, Pa took us to the tent city where Ma lives now. I think I could find it in the daytime, but it's hard to get my bearings in the dark.

In spite of my doubts, we boldly trot up the unoccupied lane. The sky's turning gray, and it won't be long before roosters crow and bunkhouses stir. Farther south, I spot a whole field of tents rising from the early mist like rows of tombstones. "That must be where the cavalry soldiers are living," I whisper to Annabelle.

By the time we come upon the two rows of wall tents occupied by the washerwomen, Annabelle and I are puffing. I count as we run down the muddy lane between the rows. "Ma's is the fourth one on the right," I tell Annabelle.

She yanks me to a stop and points. "This is the fourth."

The flap's tied shut from inside. Around me, I hear coughing, a baby's cry, and the sound of bedclothes being shook. Folks are waking, but Ma's tent is silent.

Dropping on my knees, I belly-crawl under the front. The inside of the tent is dim. "Ma?" I call hoarsely.

"Gabriel?" someone exclaims above me.

I crane my neck. Ma's standing over me, an iron skillet raised high, ready to crash on my head. Her eyes startle at the sight of me, and she sets the skillet on the ground.

"Thank the Lord I didn't strike you!" she exclaims, pressing her hand against her bodice. "I thought you were some drunken hooligan. Chile, what are you doin' here?"

Helping me to my feet, she envelops me in a hug. Her arms feel like heaven, but I pull away, thinking a man ain't supposed to be hugging his ma. "I'm here to join the other recruits," I tell her. "I know I ain't old enough to fight, but I can help in other ways."

"Pardon me!" someone hisses from outside the tent. "Gabriel?"

"Sorry." I untie the flap and a head pokes in.

"*Annabelle?*" Ma gasps. "Why on earth have you brought that poor chile with you?" she asks me in a scolding voice, as if I'd had any say in the matter.

"It's not like I invited her along," I mutter.

The opening in the tent widens, and Annabelle stoops to enter. "Oh, Missus Alexander!" she exclaims when she sees Ma. The two cling to each other, weeping.

I light a candle on an upturned box. Ma has tried to make the tent comfortable. There's fresh straw sprinkled on the dirt floor and clean quilts mounded on straw in a corner. But except for a three-legged stool and knitting needles, yarn, and a tin plate and cup on the wooden box, the tent looks the same as it did weeks ago. At least Captain Waite had made good on his promise. She didn't have to share it with seven other washerwomen.

I glance at Ma. She places one arm around Annabelle's shoulder and gestures with the other as they talk in low voices. In the candlelight, I see that her eyes are tired and her hands are red and scabby from the hot water and lye soap.

"Gabriel will escort you directly back to Woodville Farm," Ma is saying. Before Annabelle can protest, she goes on, "Is this where you want to sleep?" She gestures around the shabby tent. "Is washing dirty drawers what you want to do?"

Annabelle hesitates. I can guess how she's feeling. She had her own room in the Main House, with a four-poster bed and a chifforobe full of dresses. Granted, they were Mistress Jane's hand-me-downs, and she was always at the master's beck and call. But her duties had been laying out his suit of clothes, not washing them, and choosing the dinner menu, not cooking it. How will she fare at Camp Nelson? Poorly, I reckon, which is just what Ma's thinking.

"Annabelle, you don't belong here. This ain't the life you want. I'm only here because of Isaac." Ma cups her palm below her apron strings. "This babe needs to be born near its father. You have no reason to stay. Go back to Woodville. Let Mister Giles get you a position in town. Perhaps you can clerk for a merchant."

Annabelle drops her gaze. Throughout our journey, she's been stalwart. Now I see the weariness in her slumped shoulders.

"I told her she should go back," I say.

Ma bristles. "As should *you*, Gabriel Alexander! Last

39

letter I received, you were winning races on those horses. If you stay here, you'll be digging privies."

"I won't." I pull the telegraph from my pocket. "Captain Waite has given me permission to work with Pa and the cavalry. He says they need experienced horsemen." I hold out the telegraph, but she pushes it away.

"Only you're not a horse*man*. You're a *boy*. A boy with dreams of being a famous jockey." Tears well in her eyes.

"Ma, I still have dreams," I say. "But now they're here at Camp Nelson. After I get a bite to eat and rest for a while, I'll escort Annabelle to Woodville Farm. But I'll be back—no matter how tedious the journey—and you can't deny me."

"You can't deny me, either!" Annabelle suddenly speaks up. "I won't be returned to Woodville Farm like unwanted baggage." Bending, she reaches back through the tent opening, her hat brim catching, and an instant later drags her valise into the tent. When she straightens, she glares at Ma and me. "I'm not a slave anymore, and I won't be ordered around. I aim to make up my own mind!"

"But Annabelle, this is no life for a young lady." Using her apron, Ma dabs angrily at the tears trickling down her cheeks. "I'm sorry, Missus Alexander," Annabelle says, her voice calmer now. "I can't go back to Woodville. I know I can be of use here somehow."

Ma's fury suddenly drains. Putting an arm around each of us, she holds us close. "Then it is done. I pray the Lord will keep you safe."

Abruptly she drops her arms. "The sun is rising, and the

drums will soon tap reveille. Annabelle, hide your valise under the quilts. You'll need to work with me at the kettles. Soldiers check each tent for slackers, who are promptly removed from camp."

I look at Annabelle, hoping thoughts of boiling water and burning lye will shake her from her stubbornness. But she kneels, opens her valise, and pulls out a faded calico. "I'd best change first," she says.

Ma turns to me. "Gabriel, find your pa's tent. Ask for Company B and Sergeant Alexander."

"Sergeant?"

Pride shines in her eyes. "Your pa's deft hand with the horses has earned him a promotion." She sighs. "His sergeant's stripes were a high moment for us. But oh, Gabriel, I wish you'd stayed at Woodville Farm and stuck with the racing. Life here, well, it ain't pretty."

"Yes ma'am." There's no use arguing. I nod goodbye to the womenfolk and take my leave. After traveling day and night with Annabelle, I feel empty without her. But the lane between the tents is bustling with colored women stoking fires and ladling food from pots, so I grab my bundle and hurry off before their curiosity is roused.

I jog in the direction of the men's tents. The sun is finally peeking over the horizon, and the dew on the grass glitters like tiny jewels. On a cool summer morning like this, I'd normally be up early working Aristo. The colt would be prancing and hopping and mouthing the bit, eager to gallop.

My heart aches at the thought of never riding him again. But I know this is where I belong.

Stopping to catch my breath, I look west. I can see the Soldiers Home—where I bunked one night with Pa on my first visit—across the pike. A ways behind it are the main stables. A whinny rings across the camp and my heart catches. *Pa can wait just a bit longer to see me,* I decide as I head for the horses.

It's a hike to the four long barns, arranged in a square like the sides of a box. In the center is an arena for drills and dirt paddocks where they turn out the horses. Camp Nelson supplies food, weapons, mules, and horses for the Union troops fighting in Tennessee. When Pa first mustered in, he worked with worn-out or wounded horses called remounts. His job was to get them fit so they could return to the battlefield.

When I reach the stables, I stride through the wide doors of the closest building. A horse pokes its head over the first stall door, and I scratch between its eyes. When I pull my hand away, it's covered with dirty tufts of hair.

I glance into the second stall. This horse ain't so sociable. Its head is tucked in the farthest corner. Talking softly, I unlatch the door. My bare toes squish in the wet straw. I stroke his neck and down his chest. The horse looks as if he was once handsome and muscular. Now my fingertips ripple across every rib. His near hind leg is wrapped with gauze, and I smell the festering wound.

The war's tough on soldiers, Pa had told me, *but it's hell on horses.*

The wound needs washing and fresh wrap. The horse

needs sweet grass and grooming. And the stalls need a good mucking.

A sense of purpose fills me.

Now I know why I've been drawn to Camp Nelson. Ma and Pa need me. But so do the horses.

The tapping of drums and the trumpeting of bugles snap my attention away from the horse. I better hurry, or I'll miss Pa.

Holding my bundle under one arm, I latch the door and run from the barn. Colored soldiers are walking down the lane toward me, heading for the mess hall. As I trot past, one of them teases, "Where you goin,' boy? A Rebel after you with a whip?"

"Nah, just my ma," I josh as I scan the squad for Pa, but he ain't with this bunch. Cutting off on the lane to the right, I take a shortcut to the colored barracks, down a path behind the Soldiers Home. Next to it, farther down, is the hospital.

Across the pike, a company of soldiers is drilling in the field beside the colored barracks. The men move in a wave of blue as a lone voice rings out, "Left…left. Left, right, left." On the pike, two mounted soldiers patrol the road, stopping stragglers and checking passes. My steps falter. All I have is the telegraph from Captain Waite.

I turn tail, but not before one of the mounted guards sees me. "Halt!" he hollers, and I hear the dance of hooves.

I race for the hospital. It's a distance, but if I reach it, I can lose myself among its many wards and outbuildings. I round the back corner of the first ward and hunker behind a stack of firewood. The soldier canters his horse right by my hiding spot, but I reckon he'll be back soon for a closer look.

Behind the hospital there's a small building half-hidden in a stand of trees. I peer around the woodpile. To my left, patients in wheelchairs sit on a terrace, basking in the early morning sun. Some have bandaged limbs; others have no limbs at all. I don't see any mounted guards.

I take off for the trees, hunched low so as not to attract attention. My lungs are about to burst when I reach the outbuilding. The door's unlocked, so I rush inside. It's cool and dark, with only one small-paned window lighting the room. I shut the door and crouch behind a table, my heart pounding like the reveille drums.

Outside I hear the guard's horse trot past.

I hold my breath, listening for approaching footsteps. If I don't find Pa soon, I'll have to look for Captain Waite. Mister Giles told me that if I wish to stay at Camp Nelson, the captain would have to secure permission from the colonel of the regiment. With papers from him, I won't have to hide from every eagle-eyed sentry.

I huddle there in the shadows, waiting until I'm sure the guards have given up their search. Slowly I rise from behind the table, my eyes on that window. Nothing stirs beyond the glass panes, and I exhale with relief. As I sling my bundle over my shoulder again, my hand brushes something bristly. I drop my gaze to the top of the table, and goose bumps rise on my flesh.

A man gazes up at me, his bearded face waxy with death. Gasping, I scuttle backwards and bang into the edge of another table. I whirl. Another man lies on top, his unblinking sockets raised toward heaven. His cheeks are sunken, his arms skeletal.

Shuddering, I force myself to look around the room. Table after table holds a corpse. More are piled in a corner, like a steeple of flesh.

A scream clogs my throat.

This place is filled with the dead!

CHAPTER FIVE

Slapping my hand over my mouth, I lunge for the door, throw it open, and tear out of the building. I flee around the other side of the hospital and race blindly across the pike toward the colored barracks, all worries about that mounted guard scared straight from my mind. I glance over my shoulder, picturing dead soldiers chasing me—dry flesh flapping, brittle bones rattling—and the scream finally spews unbidden between my fingers: "Aieeeee!"

Whack! I slam into someone so hard that I bounce into the air and land on the ground. A white soldier stares down at me. He's young, with only a trace of mustache over his lip.

"P-pardon sir…I mean, C-Captain," I stammer. "Pardon for knocking into you, but…but…*g-ghosts!*" I wave wildly in the direction of the hospital.

Laughter busts out all around me, and I stop stuttering long enough to realize I'm completely encircled by colored soldiers.

One of the soldiers addresses the young officer. "Cap'n Waite, sir, I reckon this boy must've stumbled into one of the dead houses."

Two strong hands lift me from behind. "Stand up, Gabriel."

I spin around. "Pa?"

He's not laughing with the others. "Men, this young man who claims to be seeing ghosts is my son, Gabriel Alexander. Son, you remember Captain Waite. And these are the soldiers of Company B."

I lower my head, ashamed at my cowardliness.

"Don't fret, Gabriel," the captain says. "There's not a man among us who dares enter a dead house, even on a bet."

A chorus of "Amens" rings through the air.

Captain Waite suddenly turns serious. "All right, men, it's time to get a move on!" he shouts. "Attention!" The soldiers hastily assemble into even lines, all eyes to the front. Pa stands to the left, his three yellow sergeant's stripes on his sleeve. The trumpeter sounds several notes and the captain says, "Dismissed."

Most of the soldiers head off. A few stop to introduce themselves: Private Joseph Black, Private Crutcher, Private Morton, and Corporal Vaughn, who has taken over Pa's position in the squad. I shake their hands numbly.

"Welcome to Company B, Gabriel," Private Black says. "You gave us a good laugh!" Contrary to his name, Private Black is light skinned. "I'm especially pleased to meet you. My own sons are 'bout your size, and I surely miss them," he adds solemnly.

Corporal Vaughn shakes my hand last. He's fresh faced, not much older than me. His palm is uncalloused, and he wears glasses. Might be he's a scholar. "Your pa has told us much about you."

When all the soldiers have left, I finally look at Pa. His expression is stony. "What are you doing—?"

"I think I can explain," Captain Waite breaks in. "Mister Giles telegraphed me about Gabriel's decision to come to Camp Nelson. He knew the boy would need an entry into camp, and thought I could supply it. He also wrote glowingly of Gabriel's skill with horses, something sorely needed in Company B."

"Thank you, sir," Pa says. I think I detect a hint of pride in his voice, but there's a dark frown on his face. "Permission to be excused?" When the captain nods, Pa puts his hand on my shoulder and leads me a few paces away from Captain Waite. "You left Woodville Farm and jockeying?" His tone is harsh.

"Yes sir. It was time to move on."

His spine goes rigid. "Your mama and I specifically ordered you to stay at the farm."

"But, Pa, I wanted to be here with you and Ma. I want to help the Yankees fight for freedom."

"At Camp Nelson, we obey orders. We don't run away without permission."

"I *can* obey soldiers' orders. But, Pa," I protest, "I ain't a slave no more. I made up my own mind. And I didn't run away. Mister Giles gave me permission."

"Does your ma know you're here?"

"Yes sir. Annabelle and me—"

"Annabelle! You brought her, too?" Pa jerks his forage cap off his head and slaps it against his leg. I've never seen him so riled up.

"I thought you'd be pleased I was here, sir. Captain Waite believes I'll be useful."

Pa doesn't dare throw a murderous glance at Captain Waite, so he aims it at me. "Then I'll leave it to Captain Waite to decide what to do with you," he retorts, and he strides off in the direction of the mess tent.

I watch him go, wondering if I made a powerful mistake by coming to Camp Nelson.

"Sergeant Alexander seems peeved with you," Captain Waite says.

"That's for certain." I pick up my bundle and dust it off. "And I wouldn't blame you, Captain Waite, if you sent me packin' after slammin' into you like that. I wouldn't want a coward like me in Company B."

"Gabriel, you're too young to enlist in the company, but that doesn't mean you can't be useful. We have many civilians working and living at Camp Nelson."

I don't know what a civilian is, but his words sound encouraging.

"Your pa will settle down," Captain Waite says with a smile. "Especially when I assure him that the most dangerous job I'll assign you is picking out horses' hooves."

I venture a smile back. "You mean I can stay?"

"Well, Gabriel, Company B has a stable full of horses, all of them rejected by the white companies. Each soldier is assigned one horse to care for, and there are extra mounts in case of problems." He shakes his head. "And Lord knows we have problems. The colored cavalry, which barely has a name that's official, has been given the worst mounts in camp. They need grooming, doctoring, and training. Many of these nags are unbroken; some spent their lives behind plows. And others, like my own mount Champion, are like riding greased thunderbolts. They must have bucked off enough white soldiers to get themselves sent along to us."

I grin. "Sounds like Mister Giles's colt, Aristo."

"You'll need a pass from Colonel Brisbin. Right now, he's in charge of organizing the regiment, which will most likely be called the Fifth. The colonel's a well-known abolitionist who believes colored soldiers will fight as hard and valiantly as white. " He points to the field of tents on the hill. "First I'll show you where to stow your gear. You can bunk with the drummer boys."

"Thank you, sir, but a stall will do me fine."

The approaching *clip-clop* of horses' hooves draws my attention to the road. The mounted guard who chased me into the dead house is trotting toward us, his expression more peeved than Pa's.

Stopping his horse, which is still lathered from the chase, he salutes Captain Waite. "Sir, permission to throw this guttersnipe from camp."

"Permission denied, Lieutenant Wagoner. This boy is Company B's new stable hand."

The lieutenant's nostrils flare, as if he detects a bad smell. "Sir, we don't need any more coloreds in camp. There are already too many refugees and Negro soldiers. The orders from headquarters—"

"Dash headquarters," Captain Waite says. "I'll take the matter up with Colonel Brisbin."

"Yes, Captain." Lieutenant Wagoner scowls at me and then at the captain before cantering off. The lieutenant is years older than Captain Waite. I wonder how he and the other soldiers feel about taking orders from an officer so young.

"The lieutenant's from Tennessee," Captain Waite mutters, as if that explains all. I'd like to tell him I don't need no explanation. Being in the North for a while already taught me that hatred knows no borders.

Still, I'd hoped Union soldiers would be different. Ain't they fighting to free the slaves? Why then are so many of them dead set against having coloreds in camp? Then I remind myself that Captain Waite has been mighty helpful to me and my pa, and Colonel Brisbin is an abolitionist, which I gather means he cottons to black folks. At least there's a few Yankees who ain't like the lieutenant.

That thought cheers me as I follow Captain Waite. I'm in sore need of some cheering up after my less-than-cordial reunion with Pa. He'll come around, I know. I just have to convince him that I belong here with Company B.

★ ★ ★

The next morning finds me nestled in a bed of sweet-smelling straw in an empty horse stall. I'm half-asleep, my blanket over my head, when something pokes me in the side. Flinging off the blanket, I leap to my feet, fists clenched, ready to smite skeletons and corpses. Only it's just Pa, leaning on a pitchfork.

"Think you're still in Saratoga fighting those bullies?" he asks.

I shake my head sheepishly. "No sir."

"You slept through reveille and the call to breakfast." He tosses the pitchfork and I catch it by the handle. "You'll have to clean stalls on an empty stomach."

"But Pa—"

"I ain't Pa no more." He gives me a stern look. "I'm Sergeant Alexander, your superior, and you will obey orders without question. Do you understand?"

I nod.

"Company B has about sixty men, divided into squads. I'm sergeant of the 1st Squad. We've sixteen men. That's sixteen horses and sixteen stalls. You'll muck, lime, and bed them all by tonight."

"By *tonight?*"

"Without question!" he barks.

I startle. At Woodville Farm, Pa and me worked side by side every day. Never once did I hear him yell.

"Stalls will be empty this morning because we're having mounted drill. Do the mucking then. Wheelbarrow's at the end of the stable by the manure wagon. Tonight, you'll help Private Black feed the horses. He'll show you the rations. Tomorrow you'll help Private Crutcher. Make sure you rise before the sun. Any questions?"

I throw back my shoulders. "No *sir!*"

He leaves without another word.

As soon as the stall door shuts behind him, my shoulders droop. I kick my blanket into the corner. I know why Pa's acting like a drill sergeant. He's hoping I'll scurry back to Woodville Farm like a whipped dog.

Only that ain't going to work. My pass from Colonel Brisbin is in my pocket and I'm determined to be a soldier.

Thrusting the pitchfork like a sword, I attack the wall. "Take that, you Rebel vermin!"

"Whoa, boy." Private Black rests his arms on the top of the stall door. "Save that for the real graycoats."

I perk up. "We fightin' them soon?"

He laughs heartily. "Yes sir. Right after we sweep the aisles, dig the wells, and clean the privies. Oh, and learn us how to fire rifles."

"You ain't fired a rifle yet?"

"You see any rifles when we were drilling yesterday?"

I shake my head.

"Captain Waite promises us broomsticks for tomorrow's practice." Again, the private breaks into laughter, and I can't help but join him. "I've got a present for you." His eyes twinkle as he pulls something from his back pocket. It's a Yankee kepi. He tosses it on my head. "Belonged to the drummer boy."

"Thank you!" I settle the cap on my head, avoiding the question of what happened to the drummer boy.

"Now you look a real soldier."

I hear the notes of a bugle.

53

"That means 'to horse'," Private Black explains. "A good cavalryman has to learn the commands signaled by the trumpeter. Come on." He gestures for me to follow. "I'll show you 'round."

Unlatching the stall door, I jog after him. The last two soldiers are leading their mounts from the stable.

"Don't worry 'bout your pa," Private Black says as we walk down the aisle. "He's a good sergeant. The men in our squad respect him. He should be captain of Company B, but ain't no colored officers allowed. Cap'n Waite means well, but I believe that boy's just left his mama. Luckily your pa and Reverend Fee keep up our spirits. The reverend not only preaches, he works hard to get the colored soldiers supplies and respect."

I nod. "I've heard of the reverend."

"Your pa's good with the men *and* the horses," Private Black goes on. "And we do need someone who knows horses. Most of these men who used to be slaves ain't even been on a mule before."

I slip in a brag. "Pa trained racehorses."

Private Black chuckles. "No breds for the colored soldiers. Me, I've been assigned a slab-headed roan I named Hambone 'cause he's so pigheaded." He stops in front of the last stall. It has a barred top door, like a jail cell. "This here's Champion, Cap'n Waite's mount. I call him Devil."

I peer through the bars. Champion is a sixteen-hand stallion, as glossy and black as a crow except for a brilliant white star. He's a Thoroughbred, no doubt confiscated from a Rebel owner's stable. When he sees me watching him, he pins his ears and lunges, raking his teeth against the iron bars.

"That horse is rank. Cap'n Waite don't ride him enough." Private Black lowers his voice. "I believe the captain's a mite scared of him. Not that I blame him. Your pa appointed me the horse's groom 'cause of my experience. Devil here and me get along fine as long as I carry an ax handle and don't turn my back on him."

"You worked with horses before?"

"Yep. I'm a teamster. The Yankees impressed me into labor when Camp Nelson was first built, and I drove many a wagon to Tennessee. I got tired of looking at the backside of a horse, so I enlisted as soon as President Lincoln made it law."

Hooking my fingers through the bars, I study Champion. I can read a horse like Annabelle reads a book. There's a glint of fear in Champion's eyes that tells me his story: he's been whipped too many times. Now his gnashing teeth and flat ears say, "Stay away. I don't want to be hurt no more."

The horse don't need an ax handle. What he needs is a soft touch.

"I'd like to be Champion's groom," I say.

Private Black shrugs. "Far as I'm concerned, he's all yours. I'd rather be on the field drilling with my squad than tussling with that crazy animal. Only it ain't up to me."

We walk outside, where he shows me the wheelbarrow and manure wagon. A wooden ramp slants from the ground to the wagon's end gate. "Don't fill your barrow too full or you won't get it up that ramp. Now, I got one more order."

He stoops to whisper in my ear. "There's a plate of syrup-soaked cornbread hidden on top of a trunk in the saddle room, so eat up. Soldier works harder on a full belly." He winks. "Just don't tell your pa."

Private Black will be a good friend, I think when he leaves. As I pick up those wheelbarrow handles, I hear shouting on the other side of the barn. A number of saddled horses are walking two by two in the fenced area in the center of the four stables. A soldier holds the reins of each horse. I see Corporal Vaughn standing slightly apart. Pa's in the front of the arena, mounted on a handsome chestnut. I immediately recognize Hero, Mister Giles's Kentucky Saddler that he gave to Pa in thanks for saving his Thoroughbreds.

"Attention!" Pa shouts. "Stand to horse!"

Instantly, the soldiers line those horses into rows. They stand smart on the left side, right hands holding both reins below the horses' muzzles, and stare straight ahead.

All because of a command from my pa.

Pride fills my heart. I lower the wheelbarrow. Raising one stiff hand to my forehead, I salute him.

CHAPTER SIX

Five days later finds me still mucking stalls. It's evening, and the horses are in the lots. The stable's quiet as I run the last wheelbarrow full of manure up the ramp as fast as I can. It wobbles unsteadily, tips, and despite my straining, the wheelbarrow pitches into the wagon bed, along with the manure.

I curse the wheelbarrow, curse the army, curse the maggoty bread and rotten salt pork they give us to eat, and most of all, I curse the dirty stalls.

Worn out, I slump on the top of the ramp and bury my head in my arms. Pa ain't let up. Sixteen stalls a day for five days adds up to...? I search my mind, but can't find the sum. To think, it wasn't so long ago that Annabelle and me were counting up my purse winnings—over two hundred dollars, which Mister Giles put in a bank for me.

Thoughts of Annabelle make me wonder what she's doing. I ain't seen her or Ma since I left them that first day. Every night I'm so weary I drop like a feed sack into my straw bed. Perhaps a few days of washing dirty linens sent her scurrying back to Woodville Farm without a goodbye, and I won't ever see her again.

Sorry burns my eyes. The only high point these past days has been grooming Champion. The stallion should be winning races, not locked in a stall day and night. I don't officially have permission, but when I'm alone in the barn late, I slip into his stall. Humming, I brush that horse until his coat shines. I'm sorely tempted to leap on him one night and gallop him in the moonlight. But I reckon that would get me kicked out of Camp Nelson for sure.

"Gabriel? Is that *you?*" a voice calls from the bottom of the ramp.

I jerk my head from my arms. Annabelle's staring up at me, her lips parted in astonishment. I scramble to my feet, slip on the manure-slick wood, and topple head over heels to the bottom of the ramp.

"Oh! Are you all right?" Annabelle's all sympathy as she helps me to my feet. But then she wrinkles her nose and fans her face with her gloved hand. "Have you been bathing in horse droppings?"

"Ain't been bathing at all," I reply crossly, mortified that Annabelle found me a filthy stable boy instead of a proud soldier. Frowning, I pick up my kepi and whap it against my leg to shake off the dirt. "I thought you'd be long gone from here."

"Why, no!" Annabelle exclaims. "Why would you think that?"

I shrug, noticing that instead of being beaten down by scrubbing, she's bright-eyed and sweet smelling. Her hair's fashionably rolled in a bun and covered with netting; her faded calico's draped with a comely shawl. Only her dingy gloves suggest she's been working.

"Indeed, I'm having the most exhilarating time!" she declares. Waltzing back and forth beside the wagon, she gushes on and on about the camp "being splendid," as if we're conversing in a parlor instead of a stable yard.

"Annabelle," I interrupt, my voice low, "it ain't proper for a lady to be sashaying around the stables unescorted."

"For your information, I have *two* chaperones," she huffs, pointing a gloved finger over my shoulder.

I turn around. Pa and Ma are strolling beside the fence enclosing the horse paddocks, their arms linked as if they're courting.

"And your pa's your superior, so you better mind your manners," she teases, before switching the subject. "Have you met Reverend Fee? He's been running Camp Nelson School for Colored Soldiers. He's helping me establish a school in the tent city where your ma and I live." Annabelle swings to face me, her eyes glowing. "Gabriel, every day I get to teach! Not in a real schoolhouse, mind you, but in a tent just for learning. Reverend Fee has provided benches, and he's procuring books and tablets. Oh, he's a man of unlimited ambition! He's talking about building a government camp for the soldiers' families, too. Reverend Fee has such heavenly ideas that I believe he may be a saint!"

I fold my arms against my chest, listening with a doubtful and jealous heart.

Annabelle keeps bragging on and on about Reverend Fee. Finally she stops pacing. She turns to me coquettishly. "And how have you fared the past five days? Your ma and I hoped you would visit us."

My tongue sticks to the roof of my mouth. I'd love to lie and tell Annabelle I'm too busy fighting Rebels to have tea in her tent. But I've never been a liar, and I ain't going to start now. 'Sides, Annabelle can clearly tell by my shabby britches—the same ones I was wearing when we arrived—that I ain't no soldier.

Still, I don't have to let on that I'm nothing but a muck-worm. Setting the kepi on my head, I adjust it at a rakish angle. "I'm the stable hand for Pa's squad," I tell her. "I help care for their horses, so I ain't had time for social visits." I want to puff myself up even more, but I'm too yellow.

"My, that sounds like a lot of responsibility." Annabelle says, and I'm surprised there's no mockery in her voice.

"I can show you the stable," I venture, doubting she'll accept. I can count on one hand the number of times Annabelle visited the barn at Woodville Farm.

She smiles. "I'd like that."

"The horses ain't as grand as Mister Giles's Thorough-breds." As we walk down the aisle, I shy away from her, since I'm grimy from head to toe. But when we reach Champion's stall, she moves so close that her skirts brush my toes.

"Except for Captain Waite's mount, Champion, who appears h-highly bred," I stutter.

She peers through the bars. "Oh, he is so handsome!"

"As handsome as your Reverend Fee?" I blurt out the words before I can stop myself.

She slants her eyes at me, a smile playing across her lips. "Why Gabriel Alexander, I do believe I note a hint of jealousy in your voice."

My cheeks flame beneath the smudges of manure. "That's because he's all you've talked of so far!"

"Or perhaps his name was all you heard," she murmurs. "I also spoke about teaching. Every day my thoughts get stronger on the matter," she continues. "You *soldiers* may believe that fighting and killing are the way to freedom. But I believe reading and writing are more powerful. That's why white folk don't allow us to be taught. They're afraid that if coloreds are educated, we'll refuse to be kept as slaves."

I stare at Annabelle, speechless. She has no idea of the importance of the soldiers she mocks, and yet I can't find the words to argue. Why does she always render me mute like this?

Fortunately, Champion saves me from further humiliation by crashing against the door. Startled, Annabelle screams and stumbles backward, and for a moment I grasp her elbow to keep her from falling.

"My, he's rather fierce," Annabelle declares as she backs away.

"Naw, he's a lamb," I boast to hide my awkwardness. Mustering a dust-speck of courage, I say, "After I show you the horses, I'd like to walk you home. That way you can show me your teaching tent on the way."

Annabelle smiles. "I'd like that, Gabriel. You know, your ma and I have missed you. *I've* missed you," she says softly.

I stop dead in my tracks. Annabelle continues up the aisle, sashaying from one side of the aisle to the other as she peers curiously into the stalls.

I open my mouth, wanting to say that I've missed her, too. But all I can do is stare, spellbound by the tuck of her waist and the flare of her skirts as they sway with each delicate step.

★ ★ ★

The next evening I work like fury to finish those stalls. Tonight, I'm determined to see Annabelle again *and* get a glimpse of that know-it-all do-gooder Reverend Fee. Annabelle's teaching a class, and I aim to be in the first row. Not to learn, mind you, but to keep an eye on the reverend.

I've one last stall to muck, and then I'm heading to the wash tent for a bath and change of clothes. Private Black's promised me a chunk of soap and a tub of clean water, not scummy thirds.

I'm forking wet straw into the wheelbarrow so fast that I barely hear someone call my name.

"Gabriel, could you assist me?"

Without stopping my work, I glance up. Captain Waite is standing in the aisle. A saber in its scabbard hangs from his sword belt at his left side. On his right side, the grip of a revolver juts from a leather holster. Sharp spur rowels poke from the heels of his polished boots, which rise to cover his knees, and a slouch hat covers his head.

Dropping the pitchfork, I snap to attention, even though I ain't a real soldier. "Yes sir! I await your orders!"

"I need Champion tacked up, but Private Black is nowhere to be found. And I've heard enough stories from your pa to know you're right handy with a horse. He even showed me a newspaper clipping about your win in Saratoga."

I bite back a grin, pleased that he saw my name in the paper. "I'm at your service, Captain," I say, all thoughts of Annabelle wiped from my mind. Eager to get the job done before Private Black appears, I dash to the supply room. I know exactly where to find Champion's tack, since I oiled the Grimsley saddle this morning.

I slip the saddle from the rack and grab a clean blue blanket with a gold outline. Captain Waite has picked out a cumbersome bridle with two sets of reins and a bit with a high port and long curved shanks. I shudder at the sight of it. From all my work with Champion, I've learned two important things: The horse is smart and sensitive, and he reacts to pain with meanness. Sharp rowels and long shanks? No wonder he bucks.

Do I dare make a suggestion to the captain?

I think back to Pa's words from my first visit to Camp Nelson: *Most officers don't want advice from a colored man.* But then I remember something else Pa told me. *You've got to have a man's respect before you can teach him anything.* I glance at the captain, who's unbuckling a bridle strap. I gained Champion's trust and respect, so now I need to take another gamble. If I can win the captain's respect, I might not have to muck stalls forever.

I clear my throat. "Captain, sir. Permission to speak."

"Permission granted."

"I…um…it's about…it's just that—"

"If you have something to say, Gabriel, spit it out."

"Yes sir. I've been grooming Champion every night, getting to know the horse. The others call him 'Devil', but I don't agree. I might have a few ideas to help you ride—"

I cut off my words quick. Now I've done it. I've dared to suggest that an officer can't ride his own horse. I might as well join the corpses in the dead house.

Shifting his gaze from the bridle, Captain Waite says, "Go on. I'm listening."

"Y-you don't mind?"

"What I mind is looking like a fool in front of my men because I can't handle my animal. I grew up riding iron-mouthed livery nags. I know Champion is highly bred, so—"

I don't even let him finish. "Sir, Champion don't need this fierce bit." I pluck a different bridle with a snaffle bit off the hook. "He don't need spurs." I glance at the rowels on his heels. "And for tonight's ride, he don't need a scabbard slapping his belly. The horse is strong and smart, but he's flighty and tender-mouthed, like many other Thoroughbreds. He needs a gentle, confident rider."

"Well, I'll be." Captain Waite pushes back his slouch hat.

"Are you saying that all this time I've been riding him contrary to what he needs?"

"Yes sir. I mean, *no* sir. I mean, you're right. The pain is what's making the stallion buck."

"All right then, Gabriel. I guess it's worth trying it once your way." Captain Waite tosses the bridle with the curb on the top of a trunk. "Thank you for your horse sense."

"Don't thank me yet, sir. Your ride will be the proof."

"Perhaps you can join me in the paddock to guide me."

I gather this is an order, but I'm feeling nervous again as together we stride to Champion's stall. The horse flattens his ears until he sees it's me. Then he whickers, and when I go into the stall, he snuffles my hair. The sight stops the captain in his tracks.

"By golly, if I didn't see this with my own eyes, I wouldn't believe it. You've turned this devil into a kitten."

I fold the blanket into six thicknesses—just how Private Black taught me—place it on Champion's back, and flatten out the wrinkles. I slide it back, careful to smooth the horse's hair underneath. Then I heave up the saddle, adjust everything, and ease tight the girth. While I bridle Champion and lead him outside, the captain removes his spurs and scabbard.

It's dusk, and a few soldiers and stable hands are still working. As we stride toward a fenced paddock, Captain Waite and the stallion quickly attract attention. Several men jump from wagon seats and haymows; others swarm from the nearby barns. Hurrying over to the fence, they lean on the top board and begin swapping bets.

The captain sighs. "It seems the stories of my mishaps with this animal have spread through every unit."

I halt Champion in the middle of the paddock and run my hand down his neck. His muscles quiver, and his eyes are white rimmed. "The horse is riled up, Captain, so it's up to you to stay calm. That'll keep him calm, too."

"I will do my best." Gathering the reins, Captain Waite mounts. Instantly Champion throws his head and prances sideways. I talk to the horse in a low voice until he's quiet. "He may still want to buck from habit," I warn.

The captain leans down as if adjusting his stirrup. "I'm all ears. Got any last-minute advice on keeping my seat?"

"Just remember, this horse bucks because he's afraid of pain. So keep a soft hold on the reins and a light leg on his sides." I think back to when Pa taught me to ride. "Use steady aids, not jerky. And don't canter. If he even thinks about bucking, sit deep and keep him moving forward."

Captain Waite repeats all the directions. By this time, every spot along the fence is taken.

Straightening in the saddle, the captain looks around. "I believe Reverend Fee's church tent will be empty tonight. It looks as if betting, not praying, will be this evening's entertainment."

"My money's on you, Captain." I let go of the rein and step back.

Champion prances off, hooves drumming. Saliva foams as he mouths the bit. But Captain Waite rides quiet and light. Soon the wild look leaves Champion's eyes, and he's trotting around the ring with long strides.

A dozen soldiers along the rail whoop and begin collecting their winnings. Suddenly, two horses pulling a carriage careen up the lane toward the paddock. Champion startles and spins, almost tossing Captain Waite. But the captain recovers his seat, and before the horse can leap into a buck, he legs him forward.

The driver halts the carriage. Two soldiers sit in back, and I can tell by the eagle epaulets on the shoulders of one of them that he's a colonel. The other man, who has the one bar of a lieutenant, jumps from the carriage, salutes Captain Waite, and motions him over. "Colonel Brisbin needs to relay some urgent news," he calls.

Captain Waite trots Champion to the gate, and I grab the horse's bridle. The captain dismounts and salutes the colonel as he approaches the carriage.

"Exciting news, Captain Waite," Colonel Brisbin says from his carriage seat. "I've already alerted Companies D and H. On orders from General Burbridge, the soldiers of the colored cavalry will soon be engaged in battle!"

CHAPTER SEVEN

Captain Waite's success on Champion has changed life for me at Camp Nelson. I am now Private Gabriel Alexander, assistant to the captain and Champion's groom. I'm not a real private, seeing as I'm still too young to muster in. But I'm wearing the drummer boy's blue uniform, and the men in Pa's squad call me "Private Gabriel."

And Colonel Brisbin's recent news has changed life for everyone. The colored cavalry soldiers are preparing to march to Virginia!

For the past two days, there's been a flurry of drilling with rifles and preparing horses. Blacksmiths are working round the clock to make sure the mounts are well-shod for the journey. Teamsters have been loading up the supply and ammunition wagons and readying the mules. Harness makers are busy repairing bridles, saddles, and harnesses.

When I'm not caring for Champion, I'm assisting Captain Waite. I'm delivering messages, fetching supplies, and dogging his heels in case he needs me to run an errand.

The third morning after Colonel Brisbin's announcement, I accompany the captain to the colonel's office.

"Wait for me in the hall, Gabriel," Captain Waite orders. He strides into Colonel Brisbin's office, leaving the door ajar. Sliding closer, I peek through the crack between the frame and the door.

"My men are working hard to get ready," Captain Waite is saying to the colonel. "But they're constantly assigned privy duties by commanders of the white regiments, despite the order from the War Department. That doesn't leave us enough time to drill. Some of my soldiers are still learning right from left. And this week, we've just commenced mounted drill on horses that are barely half-broke. I fear that we will not be prepared for the rigors of battle."

"You have no choice, Captain," Colonel Brisbin says. "On General Burbridge's orders, the colored cavalry will march in three days."

Three days! Since I'm planning on traveling with Company B, that means I'll soon be leaving, too—and I've yet to be assigned a horse or a pair of boots!

"That's little time," Captain Waite points out.

"Are you saying the colored troops aren't worthy of this endeavor?" Colonel Brisbin asks.

Captain Waite draws himself to full height. "No sir. They are wholly raw, but more than worthy. I have this week taught them to load-in-the-nine-times. Most have never held a weapon, yet they perform better than the white company I commanded."

Sensing the pride in his words, I straighten my spine, too.

Colonel Brisbin nods. "That's what I want to hear, Captain. The prejudices against Negro soldiers can only be dispelled by their conduct on marches, in battle. And, of course, in retreat." He casts a grave eye on Captain Waite. "I don't believe I need to remind you of Fort Pillow?"

Captain Waite grimaces. "No sir. That tragedy does not need to be repeated."

Fort *Pillow?* The only pillow I know is the straw one under my head at night.

"General Burbridge is leading several brigades to Saltville, Virginia," the colonel continues. "Once there, the army's objective is to destroy the saltworks. Colonel James Wade and I will command a colored cavalry regiment from Camp Nelson. From this point on, it will be unofficially called the Fifth. We'll meet Burbridge's troops at Preston-burg, where the regiment will be assigned to Colonel Ratliff's brigade. I expect the highest conduct from the soldiers at every point."

"I have every confidence that all of them will perform valiantly, sir." Captain Waite clears his throat. "Sir, I need to bring one more problem to your attention."

Colonel Brisbin begins to leaf through a stack of papers on his desk, as if the captain was already dismissed.

"The soldiers have been issued Enfield rifles."

The colonel doesn't look up. "I realize that, Captain. Unfortunately, they are the only available weapons. Tomorrow afternoon, supplies for the journey will be allotted.

Squad leaders will be in charge of handing them out to the soldiers."

"Yes sir." Captain Waite salutes and strides from the office. He's walking so fast, I have to jog to keep up. "Captain Waite, I'm going with Company B, right?" I ask eagerly.

He glances down at me as we walk. "That's my intention, Gabriel Alexander."

"Then, sir, won't I need a horse?"

"Speak to Lieutenant Rhodes. I'm sure he can assign you one that no one else cares to ride."

I grin. Soon I'll be a mounted soldier! Of course, I'll be a soldier without scabbard or weapon, but it's a start. "Sir, what's an Enfield rifle?"

"A cussed poor choice of arms for a cavalryman."

"And what's Fort Pillow?"

"An incident that I prefer not to discuss for the sake of my men's morale." Captain Waite halts. "Gabriel, as my assistant you are at times privy to confidential information. Fort Pillow is not to be mentioned to the others. Do I make that clear?"

Surprised by his seriousness, I nod furiously.

"Now, take this message to your pa and Lieutenant Rhodes. The trumpeter will sound "boots and saddles" in one hour. We have much to do."

"Yes sir!" Repeating the message to myself, I run off, tucking the name Fort Pillow in the back of my mind. I can tell by the captain's grim tone that it's a place I need to remember.

★ ★ ★

The next evening, I'm in Pa's wedge tent, which he shares with Private Black, Corporal Vaughn, and Private Crutcher. Supplies have been handed out, and they're arranged on the bedrolls. Pa's stooped on his side of the tent, packing some items in his knapsack. I haven't spoken to him yet about going with the company, but I'm sure Captain Waite has mentioned it.

"Cartridge box, bayonet, cup, tobacco." Private Black lists off the supplies lined up on his blanket. I kneel next to him, watching in rapt attention. On my feet are my new brogans. The stiff leather pinches my toes and blisters my heels, but I've polished them until they shine.

Picking up a cavalry gauntlet, which is a fancy name for a glove, I try it on. My hand swims in it.

"Knife, spoon, long johns, canteen, rounds of ammunition—" Private Black chuckles. "Not that we'll be doing any shooting."

"Why's that?" I ask. "Is it on account of those 'cussed Enfield rifles'?" I repeat Captain Waite's sentiments.

He laughs. "You hit that nail on the head."

"Enfield rifles are too long to be loaded while on horseback," Pa explains. "Most cavalry use carbines."

"Which means the colored cavalry soldiers will be fighting on foot, hand to hand with the enemy." Picking up his bayonet, Private Black makes a thrusting motion.

"Kill that Rebel!" I cheer him on.

Pa shoots a frown at Private Black. "Don't encourage the boy. His ma'll fret enough when she finds out he's going with us."

"She shouldn't worry. Odds are we won't see a lick of fighting," Private Black grumbles. "The only reason Burbridge is bringing us coloreds along is to clean the other troops' horses." He pretends to stick the bayonet in the dirt floor. "We'll prob'ly be using this for a tent pin."

"Oh, it might come in handy for picking hooves or cracking hardtack." Pa nods at me. "You best go see your ma tonight, Gabriel, and bid her farewell. Tomorrow will be hectic, and the next day we march at sunrise. Annabelle's expecting you, too. She says you failed to visit as promised."

My face heats up under my kepi.

"Whoo-wee. I believe someone has a sweetheart," Private Blacks joshes.

"Naw," I mutter, avoiding his eyes.

He sniffs the air. "Might be you need to clean up a bit, otherwise she'll think some ol' hog has come calling. When was your last bath? Five nights ago?"

"He can forget about bathing," Pa says. "Every soldier in camp wants a bath before marching out, so the wash tents have lines twenty soldiers deep."

"I hear Hickman Creek's not too cold and muddy." Winking, Private Black tosses me a rag and a chunk of soap.

I catch them and stand up. I've a clean shirt, thanks to Corporal Vaughn, whose penmanship has earned him a place in charge of supplies. Pa puts his arm around my shoulder and leads me outside the tent. "Gabriel, I ain't agreeing with your idea to go with Company B. But I ain't disagreeing, neither. Captain Waite assures me you'll always be behind the lines. A battle ain't no place for a boy."

He must see the protest in my eyes, because he raises one hand. "Let me finish. Since you've been at Camp Nelson, you've conducted yourself as a man. I'm right proud of you."

I've been waiting to hear those words. "Thanks, Pa."

He laughs. "You've made quite a name for yourself, too. After your first ride on Sassy, the name 'Private Gabriel' is on every soldier's tongue."

I wince. Lieutenant Rhodes has assigned me the most waspish mare that ever graced a barn. Neither man nor horse can tolerate her, so she's tethered alone. The mare tore a hunk from my arm when I saddled her, and refused to open her mouth for the bit. Then when I stuck my foot into the stirrup to mount, she ran off and left me flat on the ground, much to the delight of every soldier in Company B. I had to have Pa hold her bridle—as if I was a dainty belle first learning to ride—before I could get on the mare. And worst of all, she's gray. No cavalryman wants a gray horse, because it's too hard to keep clean.

"Now wash up and go say goodbye to your mama. Be prepared for weeping," Pa warns.

I hurry off. The rows of tents are busy with soldiers stooped over cook fires and washbasins. Some of the men are sitting on wooden boxes, cleaning rifles and boots. Others lounge on the ground, playing cards and reading Bibles. From one corner of the camp, the breeze brings both the mournful sound of a flute and the joyous sound of a harmonica. Seems I'm not the only one with mixed feelings about this journey to Virginia.

My thoughts are jangled, just like when I left Woodville Farm. Part of me is ready to meet the enemy. So far, life in Camp Nelson has been one long chore. After all the shoveling and hauling, a spell of marching and fighting sounds like a real adventure. But a small part of me ain't excited about leaving Ma, Annabelle, and Kentucky for a place far over the mountains.

Still another part of me longs for Aristo, Captain, Sweet Savannah, and Tenpenny. It's been many days since I left Woodville Farm. *Is Jackson winning races on Aristo?* I wonder. *Has Short Bit proven himself as a rider?* I'm surrounded by horses here, but the joy of training and racing those Thoroughbreds will never leave me.

As I walk toward the creek, I also think about Annabelle. I never did get to meet her Reverend Fee. I guess my pinch of jealousy got pushed aside by thoughts of war. Still, I'm excited to see her tonight, even though our meeting will be a farewell. At least I'll be saying goodbye in a uniform.

Hickman Creek is a few yards beyond the washerwomen's steaming kettles and drying lines. I doubt they're working this late in the evening, but when I reach the winding stream, I hunt for a private spot to bathe. Contrary to what Private Black heard, the water's muddy—probably men are watering their horses up creek. But I find a spot that's fairly clear and strip to the waist. I wash my arms and shoulders, shivering the whole while. Modesty keeps me from washing further.

I slide into the clean shirt, place my kepi over my damp hair, and then button up my jacket. It ain't as fancy as Pa's: He wears a woolen jacket trimmed with yellow braid. But it ain't as plain as the fatigue jackets worn by most of the cavalrymen. When I fasten my last button, I can't help but stand tall.

Half-clean, I hike to Ma and Annabelle's tent. It's empty. An old black lady points to a large walled tent set apart from the others. "The young one's teachin' tonight," she says, and I thank her.

As I approach the tent, I can hear Annabelle's voice. "Scholars, open your primers to…"

The flaps are pulled back and tied. I peek through the triangular opening. Two kerosene lanterns hanging from poles illuminate the tent. Its canvas walls bulge, and every bench is filled with soldiers in blue, women in headscarves, and workers in homespun. All heads are bent as they follow Annabelle's directions.

I hesitate for a moment, then slip into the tent. I scoot onto the end of a bench, whispering, "Pardon me, 'scuse me," until the others slide over a hair to make room. I glance down the row, noting there's one primer for the five of us on the bench.

"Scholars, I will hold up a card with a letter. Point to the letter in the primer and repeat after me: *A.*"

I crane my neck, trying to glimpse Annabelle over the forest of heads. But I can only see the card. As she holds more up, I repeat the letters along with the others. The lesson seems to drone on forever.

"Scholars, these letters make up words," Annabelle says. "And the words become the sentences that we read in the Bible and in letters from home."

Someone next to Annabelle holds up a card with words written on it. I sit up straight and see that the person is Ma. "Every night we will learn more letters and two words," Annabelle goes on. "Tonight's words" —she points to the cards— "are HOPE and FREEDOM. *Hope* is what we need to keep up our spirits during this war. *Freedom* from bondage is what we *hope* to gain, so we can live in dignity. Now say them with me."

Reluctantly I pronounce the words along with the others. Over and over, *hope* and *freedom* ring through the tent in a chorus. Slowly, feet begin to drum and palms begin to slap. Despite my impatience to see Ma and Annabelle, my heart soars with the voices. I do believe that one day freedom *will* be for all.

When the lesson is over, I push up front. But Annabelle's talking to a serious man wearing a stiff black suit, so I make my way over to Ma.

"It's about time you visited, Gabriel Alexander," Ma scolds with a smile. But then she sees my uniform, and her happiness fades. Her eyes bloom with tears. "No, you *can't* go with your pa... I won't let you go!"

I take her hands in mine. They're as dry as husks from long hours of washing and scrubbing. "Ma, what was all that talk about *hope* and *freedom?*" I ask. "Are they only for white soldiers to fight for?"

She shakes her head, unable to speak.

"If they want freedom, coloreds are going to have to march into battle, too," I say, only my words don't help. Ma lifts her apron to her face, and her shoulders heave with sobs. When she finally catches her breath, she says, "Gabriel, you believe this war will bring victory and freedom. But, chile, I hear the stories. All it's bringing is death."

"Ma," I sigh. "Captain Waite has promised that I won't be in harm's way." Then I add in a low voice, "I ain't going to get killed."

Calming some, she hugs me. I notice I've grown taller these days from all the hard work—and maybe from my new shoes. Peering over Ma's shoulder, I see that Annabelle's watching us, her gaze curious, as she stands with the man in the suit.

Annabelle brings the man over, and Ma lets me go. "Gabriel," Annabelle says, "I'd like you to meet Reverend John Fee."

The man nods at me seriously, holding his Bible, and I realize with relief that he's no ladies' man. As I shake his hand, I shift my gaze back to Annabelle. She's hiding a teasing smile behind her fingers, which for once are not gloved. They're as red and raw as Ma's.

When Annabelle sees me looking, her cheeks flush and

she snaps her hands behind her back. "Reverend Fee has been gracious enough to provide primers," she says hastily.

"Yes, but the lessons are prepared and executed by Miss Annabelle," the reverend says. "I have confidence in her gifts as a teacher. And I have great trust in your father as a leader," he adds, with an acknowledging nod to Ma. "I hear his unit will soon be marching."

I puff out my chest. "Yes sir, and I aim to march with them."

Annabelle blanches. Turning away, she busies herself with gathering primers.

"I will pray for the soldiers every night," the reverend says. "It was nice to meet you, Gabriel Alexander."

A group of women has clustered around Ma and Annabelle, so when the minister leaves, I hurry after him. Fort Pillow is on my mind.

"Reverend, might I have a word with you?" I ask, trying to sound like a grown man.

"Yes, Gabriel. How can I help you?"

"Can you tell me anything about Fort Pillow?"

His brow furrows and he shakes his head sadly. "A terrible massacre. The newspaper reported three hundred Negroes slaughtered by Confederate soldiers."

Massacre? Slaughtered? My breath catches in my throat.

"And for no cause." The reverend sighs. "The fort had surrendered. The Union soldiers had lain down their arms. The Rebels should have taken the colored soldiers as prisoners of war, not killed them on sight. The night I read the news of Fort Pillow was the first night I ever questioned my faith. We must all pray that such a terrible thing shall never happen again." Still shaking his head, the minister continues on his way, disappearing into the dark.

A chill races up my spine as I duck back into the yellow glow of the tent. No wonder Captain Waite refused to tell me about Fort Pillow. No wonder he made me promise to keep my silence. No soldier could march bravely into battle carrying visions of a massacre along with his rifle.

CHAPTER EIGHT

Annabelle pretends she doesn't see me when I enter the tent again. Starting from the back, I make my way down a row, picking up primers. She's purposefully avoiding me, keeping benches between us. I dart up the aisle and block her way.

"Excuse me, Gabriel," she says. "I must finish my work."

"And I will gladly help."

"I don't need your help!" Sticking her nose in the air, Annabelle whirls in a wave of calico and hurt feelings, then hurries in the opposite direction.

I follow her, not ready to give up. "I enjoyed your lesson," I say. "The words *hope* and *freedom* will forever stay in my mind."

"I'm glad," she murmurs. "Perhaps you could attend another lesson."

"My company will be leaving soon," I say. "Perhaps at the next lesson we could learn the word *goodbye*. Soldiers arrive and depart from here like it's a train depot."

Without looking at me, Annabelle silently stacks books

in my arms. We work this way until my arms get tired and I begin to lose patience. "Conversation might make the work go faster," I suggest.

"Not if the conversation is about someone leaving to *fight*," she says. She's trying to sound curt, but she just sounds upset. "Yesterday I received a letter from Mister Giles. Your pa wrote him about your ma returning to Woodville Farm after the babe is born." She touches my arm. "Gabriel, Mister Giles is eager for all of us to return. He wants me to help him with his correspondence and you to jockey his horses. We could leave tonight if need be!"

I shake my head firmly. "Might be I'll go back home after the battle at Saltville," I tell her. "But not now. I can't leave Pa, Private Black, Captain Waite, and the others. The soldiers in 1st Squad, well, they're like family."

Annabelle stares at me with such confusion that I know she don't understand. Might be I don't understand either how the soldiers of Company B have become more than just comrades.

Setting the books on a bench, I grasp her elbow. "I won't be gone forever," I say. "And I won't be in battle. I'll be behind the lines. I may wear a uniform, but I don't even carry a rifle."

She blinks, her eyes glimmering with tears. "And you believe that will keep the Rebels from killing you?"

I open my mouth to reply, but the reverend's words stop me: *The fort had surrendered.* I know I can't chase away her doubts.

"That's what I thought." Annabelle picks up the stack. Staggering under the load, she starts up the aisle, and once again my farewell remains unspoken.

Only this time, I decide, *I ain't leaving without a proper farewell.* Throwing back my shoulders, I stride up the aisle in my squeaky new brogans. If tomorrow I'm marching to Saltville to face murderous Rebels, then tonight I should be able to march up to Annabelle and face the storm of her sorrow.

★ ★ ★

The morning sun rises as red as blood. Not a favorable omen, I tell myself as I loop the webbed surcingle over my saddle. The gloomy sky could foretell a vicious battle. Or it could mean that Sassy will kick my head wide open before I even mount her.

Bending down, I reach under the mare's belly to retrieve the end of the webbed belt and bring it up so I can buckle it. She kicks out, but I made sure before I started that we were far from the other horses. Her hooves harmlessly pelt the air.

All around me, the men of the hastily formed Fifth are preparing to ride out. Traveling with the regiment are farriers to shoe the horses and veterinarians to heal them. A train of mules packed with supplies snakes down toward the road. An ammunition wagon and a supply wagon, both pulled by teams of mules, plod along at the rear of the train.

Captain Waite and several other company commanders are already mounted. They ride through the throngs, delivering orders and rallying the troops. For a moment, I watch as Champion trots by. His neck and tail are arched as he carries himself and his rider in high style. Preparing to ride into battle suits the stallion.

Turning my attention back to Sassy, I double-check the blanket roll strapped behind my saddle. Secured on top are a poncho, an overcoat, a lariat, and a lead strap. Next I look through my right saddlebag to make sure I've packed a currycomb, brush, and hoof pick, and then I check my horseshoe pouch for extra shoes and nails. They say the infantry marches on its stomach and the cavalry marches on its horse. Our lives may depend on our mounts, and I aim to take good care of Sassy and Champion.

In my left saddlebag are three days' rations for Sassy and me. I've also rigged a coffeepot onto the back of the saddle, on orders of Captain Waite, who loves his morning cup. When I lead Sassy forward, the pot clatters.

Panicking, she kicks out again and sets the coffeepot to rattling even louder. But I notice Sassy ain't the only fractious critter. All around me, horses and soldiers dance awkwardly, and cussing courses through the squads. Some of the cavalrymen bought too much from the camp sutlers yesterday and have overloaded their horses. I see bulky quilts and heavy mess kettles strapped to bedrolls, and cans of food and Bibles poking out from stuffed saddlebags.

Our squad had only two chances to drill with the Enfield rifles. The soldiers carry them in slings, and they hang awkwardly from their shoulders. Pa says the rifle alone weighs about eleven pounds, and forty rounds of ammunition weigh about six. I wonder how long it will take for the extra supplies to grow too burdensome.

Pa moves silently among his squad, checking straps, tightening girths, and calming soldiers and their mounts. He stops to show Corporal Vaughn how to fold his saddle blanket and smooth out every wrinkle to spare the horse's back. When Pa sees me watching him, he sends an encouraging smile.

My lips are too parched to smile back, so I nod a reply. My heart's pattering at the thought of this journey. I'm glad when the trumpeter sounds "to horse" and it's time for Pa and me and the other soldiers to line up.

As first sergeant, Pa calls the roll. Then Captain Waite orders us to count fours in each platoon. When all the rows, or ranks, are arranged in groups of four, he hollers, "Prepare to mount!"

We all turn to the right, let go of the reins with our right hands, step forward two paces, and face the saddle. Then, left hands holding the reins, we take hold of the pommel and put the toe of our left boots in the stirrups, ready for the next command.

Just as the captain shouts "Mount!" two companies jog past, scabbards, bridles, and rifles jangling. Our horses ain't never seen such crowds or heard such noise, and several of them start wheeling. Others rear in place, setting off the whole company. Soldiers pitch backward and toes get hooked in stirrups. A few men manage to mount, but their rifles, which they've seldom practiced with, swing into their horses' rumps, and the animals lunge forward, as if spurred.

At that point, saddles tip sideways and blankets slip from

under too-loose girths. Coffeepots and kettles clang. Next to me, a quilt flaps from a poorly secured bedroll, and Sassy decides she's had enough of the confusion. Throwing up her head, she flies backwards between the horses and riders behind me. Running with her, I turn her head and guide her into a circle. "Pardon!" I yell, but most of the soldiers don't care because they're fighting their own mounts.

When Sassy realizes she's been bested, she quits. I pat her soothingly, keeping clear of her nipping teeth, then lead her forward into rank.

The bugle blasts wildly. "Stand to horse!" Captain Waite hollers, red-faced with frustration. Slowly, the haphazard clots of men and horses organize themselves into rows that look like dark, even stripes.

I'm sweating and panting already, and we ain't even left the stable yard.

Finally Company B is mounted.

"Form ranks!" Captain Waite commands, and we trot by fours down the pike to the large field beside the colored barracks where the entire regiment is assembling.

Company B numbers about sixty soldiers and their mounts. I've heard there are 600 men in all marching today. Soldiers and horses stretch in rows up and down the pike and fill the hillside. It's an impressive sight.

It seems as if we're waiting in the sun forever. I glimpse Colonels Wade and Brisbin off at the front of it all. They're surrounded by other mounted officers and the chief trumpeter. At last Colonel Wade gives a command. He signals with his saber, and the field officers obey and repeat the command. Still, it takes a while for the regiment to move. Sassy's about to protest with a buck when we start south down the pike, four abreast.

By the time Pa's squad has traveled to the entry gate of Camp Nelson, we're riding in a cloud of dust. Pulling a handkerchief from my saddlebag, I wrap it around my nose. All around me, soldiers are doing the same. We look like a band of masked guerrillas.

I am the fourth man in my rank. Private Black rides on my left on his horse Hambone; Private Murphy rides on his left on Sherman. First man in the rank is Private Crutcher, a freed slave and shoemaker, astride Whistler.

Private Murphy's not much older than me. He enlisted only a month ago. The first time he ran away from his owner, he was caught, jailed, returned, and whipped. The scars on his back still look ugly and raw. The second time he ran away, he made it to a recruiting station in Lexington. This time, the Union soldiers didn't hand him over. Now he sits his horse like a man. Beside us on our left, Pa rides on Hero. The ranks and files of his squad are straight, and our horses paced at the correct distance.

Pride fills me as the mounted troops stamp over Wernwag Bridge, which crosses the Kentucky River at the south end of Camp Nelson. Sassy breaks into a jig as the air drums with the echo of hooves. The guards all shout "Hurrah!" as we pass.

Our journey to Saltville has begun.

★ ★ ★

My Dearest Mother,

September 24 we reached Prestonburg, Kentucky. Our regiment has been assigned to a brigade commanded by Colonel Robert Ratliff of the 12th Ohio Cavalry. In all, General Burbridge commands a force of 5,000 men. We march for Saltville in three days. Salt is important to the Rebels, and if we can destroy the saltworks, we will hit them where it hurts the most—in their rations, and their bellies. However, I hear talk that Burbridge has not been a popular general. I hope this march is not a fool's errand to boost a vain man's career and reputation.

Since we left Camp Nelson, the soldiers of Company B have performed their duties with utmost diligence, despite their lack of training and their brief time to prepare. I am honored to command them.

Tomorrow we march through Pikesville. I send you all my love and hope that this cruel war will soon be over so we can be reunited. I long to once again sit with the family by the fireside, and converse about matters other than war. Please give Father, George, and all at home my fondest greetings.

Your Son in Faith,
D. Henry Waite, Capt.

Dear Ma and Annabelle,

Captain Waite is writing these words for me, but they are my thoughts. We rode for too many days in heat and dust, camping under the stars at night. We met up with several brigades at Prestonburg. All are mounted. Unlike the 5th, most regiments have fought together in many skirmishes. The 30th Kentucky Mounted is especially a sight to behold. All their horses are white and they shine from grooming and good feed. When they march past, we stare in awe.

The 5th is the only colored regiment on this march. We've joined the 11th Michigan and 12th Ohio cavalry regiments. The white soldiers delight in taunting us. Coloreds can't fight, they say. They're cowardly slaves. One night the men of the 11th swiped about ten of our bridles and hung them high in trees. I and a few other nimble soldiers had to climb like squirrels to retrieve them.

Today we marched through Pikesville. A small party of Rebels attacked the front lines, but do not worry, Ma—the 5th saw no fighting. The soldiers in my squad have kept up their spirits with singing, joshing, and prayers. Pa rallies us well. He tells us we are marching for freedom, not for the white soldiers' praise. Captain Waite continues to treat me fair, and I have made friends with several privates. Private Black has two sons about my age. He misses them dearly. I am proud to be marching with them all.

Tomorrow Sept. 26th we cross into Virginia and head over the mountains. I hope you are both well. Keep us in your prayers,

All my Love, Gabriel

★ ★ ★

Hear that mournful thunder,
Roll from door to door,
Calling home God's soldiers,
Get home, men, go home.

Private Black's deep voice booms in front of me. It's pitch black and raining hard, and his singing guides the way.

Behind me, Private Murphy's higher voice rises along with Private Black's.

See dat forked lightning,
Flash from tree to tree,
Callin' home God's soldiers,
Get home, men, go home.

As if joining in the chorus, a bolt streaks the sky, and Sassy jigs forward. Company B is one long line of soaked horses and riders as we pick our way along a narrow mountain trail, all proper distance and order abandoned in our misery. Sassy's nose is in Hambone's tail, and Private Murphy's horse Sherman bumps against Sassy's rump, but she's too tuckered to kick.

I'm hunched in my saddle, rain dribbling down my neck and pooling under my poncho. General Burbridge has driven us all night, trying to make up for lost time. Captain Waite called it folly, but Pa said even a general could never have predicted the treacherous trail, the wicked thunderstorm, and the Rebel militia dropping trees in our path. Troops walk ahead, clearing the trees, but it's taken a toll on our march.

The trail into the mountains is narrow, so before we started the climb, the muleteers unloaded the wagons and mules. Then they emptied the horse feed into smaller sacks and distributed them among the cavalrymen. Now each man must bear the added weight of extra rations behind his saddle. Mules carry the wheels and barrels of the six small cannons called Mountain Howitzers. The wagons and their teams stayed behind in Kentucky while we forged ahead.

As we climb, the sun sets and the dark clouds break. The Kentucky soldiers who know the land have been speaking in hushed voices about these mountains. They say if the Rebels don't kill us, the mountains will. I believe they're right. The horses strain with each step, and in the roughest places we dismount and lead them to spare their strength. To lighten the burden, soldiers discard anything they can do without. Soon sodden quilts and mud-splattered food cans litter the sides of the trail. The rain is falling so hard, I can barely see Hambone's rump.

Thunder cracks and lightning illuminates the mountainside. My eyes snap wide. Beside me, so close that my left stirrup scrapes against it, is a steep wall of rock. But below my right stirrup I see *nothing* when the sky lights up again. No ground, no trees, no footing. Just a steep drop into blackness.

A shiver races through me, and I mumble prayers to help me relax. Sassy's jumpy enough. One misstep and we'll both pitch over the edge to our deaths. Earlier, word was passed back the line to "stay on the trail." But it seems the trail is fading into a trace.

As if sensing my distress, Private Black's voice again bellows comfortingly through the driving rain.

> *O, I was lost in the wilderness,*
> *King Jesus hand me the candle down.*
> *So blow your trumpet, Gabriel.*

Private Murphy chimes in.

> *O, blow your trumpet, Gabriel,*
> *Blow your trumpet—*

Private Murphy's voice abruptly cuts off. I hear a scuffle, a thump, and then a clatter, like rocks sliding off the trail.

Turning, I peer curiously over my shoulder. A bolt of lightning rends the sky, casting a ghostly brightness on the path. Sherman's still plodding behind me, his head bobbing, his mane dripping. But his saddle is empty.

Private Murphy is gone!

CHAPTER NINE

I yank on Sassy's bit, stopping her in her tracks. "Pa!" I scream. "Halt the squad! Private Murphy's off his horse!"

"What do you mean 'off his horse'?" Pa hollers, three ahead of me.

I strain my eyes, trying to see through the driving rain. Sherman looks wet but unhurt. Yet there's no shadow of a young cavalryman beside him, clinging to a stirrup on the right or hugging the wall on the left. "I mean, *he's gone!*"

Then I hear a yell from below. "Help, down here!"

"I think he fell over the edge!"

Instantly Pa's at my right stirrup, holding onto Sassy's mane to keep from toppling off the trail himself. "Sweet Jesus," he says as dirt and pebbles dislodge from beneath his boots and rattle down the steep drop-off.

Again, a cry for help rises from below.

By now, word of the accident has traveled along the entire squad. The column has stopped. Someone has passed a torch to Private Crutcher, and it sheds a golden glow.

"We'll need lariats," Pa says. He's carrying his, so I untie mine and hand it to him. "Gabriel, you're the smallest." His gaze is on the knots. I swallow hard, knowing what he will say next. "We'll lower you down. You'll need to tie the ropes around Private Murphy so we can draw him up."

"Yes sir," I say, in as brave a voice as I can muster.

"I need two men!" Pa calls. "Men who can keep their wits and their balance. Others stay mounted and calm. We don't need another fall." The orders echo up and down the path. Seconds later, Black and Crutcher have inched their way to us, lariats in hand. Pa ties the ropes together and then loops one end securely around Sassy's pommel. My life will be in the hands of three trustworthy men—and one peevish mare.

I dismount carefully, searching for a bare spot in front of Sassy where I can stand. Pa ties one end of the lariat around my waist and under my arms like a harness. Then he gives me a grave nod. "We'll play out the rope slowly. Don't worry if you slip. We'll keep hold."

"Yes sir." Taking off my kepi, I hand it to Pa. He tucks it solemnly in his waistband. Rain pelts my bare head.

No one says that this is foolish—as risky as a night march over the mountains—because we hear Private Murphy again, pleading this time. We know there is no choice.

"God be with you, Gabriel," Private Black says.

Turning, I kneel and begin a backward descent over the trail's edge, my gloved fingers scrabbling at roots and jutting rocks. Immediately, I begin to slide. The leather soles of my brogans cannot find a hold on the muddy mountainside.

Faster and faster I fall, my elbows and knees bouncing against jagged rocks and twisted roots. Fear of the dark below makes my heart pound in my chest. Above me, I hear the grunts of the men as they struggle to hang onto the rope. Finally, just as my heart is about to burst, my shoes hit the solid ground of a rock ledge and I land hard.

"Over here!" Private Murphy calls. I glance left. Thunder rolls across the mountains, and the sky flickers like a candle flame. I see his face a few feet away. He's hugging the mountainside with one arm, his cheeks white with pain. His other arm hangs limp. His poncho is hooked on an outcropping, which must have kept him from falling farther. "I think my arm's broken," he says through gritted teeth.

"I found him!" I yell up to the others. "Keep hold until I can reach him!" Taking a deep breath, I tap my foot to the left, feeling for ground firm enough to support my weight. Slowly, I edge over to Private Murphy. When I reach him, I tell him what we must do. He nods weakly.

I take off my gloves and thrust them up inside my jacket. With trembling fingers I loosen the rope, slip out of it, and then tie it around his waist and shoulders. When I yank the knots tight, he winces.

"Pull him up!" I holler. The rope goes taut. Inch by inch Private Murphy is dragged upward. I unsnag his poncho and try to boost him from below. Soon all I can see are his boots. Then, suddenly, I realize I am utterly alone.

Thunder rumbles around me. Rain patters against my poncho. Closing my eyes, I press my cheek against the wet rock, afraid to look down. *The Lord must be on the side of the*

Confederates, I think, *since he seems to be doing everything in his power to keep us from reaching Saltville.* One foot slips, but I manage to hang on. *If I fall backward off this ledge,* I wonder, *will I plunge forever into nothingness?*

The thought makes me dizzy.

"Dear Jesus, my life is in your hands," I murmur.

"Gabriel! Call out your position! We're dropping the lariat!"

I holler loud enough to wake bears in their caves. A shower of pebbles rains down, then something whacks me on the top of my head. I reach up and grasp the end of the lariat. The motion makes me sway unsteadily.

I will myself not to fall. Body trembling with fatigue, I snake the rope around my waist. My fingers are so stiff that the knots don't come easy. Finally, it's secure. Raising both arms, I grip the rope and yell, "Ready!"

Bit by bit, the lariat lifts me until my feet no longer touch the ledge. I dangle and twist in the cold rain. A rush fills me and I'm light as a bird in the air, but then my knuckles scrape against rough rock. My cheek smacks against a crag, and the stab of pain reminds me that if the knots don't hold, I won't fly like a bird.

The glow of the torch greets me first. Then I hear encouraging voices and feel strong hands under my arms. They drag me onto an empty bit of trail in front of Sassy's legs. My cheek and chest are bruised, and the skin of my palms and fingers is rubbed raw. For a moment, I curl in a ball and press my body joyously to the level ground.

Pa kneels beside me, looking mighty worried. Water drips from the brim of his forage cap.

"Is Private Murphy going to be all right?" I ask.

Looking relieved, Pa helps me to a sitting position. "The surgeon will have to set his arm," he says.

I lean my back against the cliff. Pa pulls my kepi from under his jacket and places it back on my head. "You did well, Private Gabriel."

"Thank you, sir." Sassy dips her head and blows at my cap, as if inspecting me for injuries.

"Your horse stood fast," Pa says. "She knew what was expected of her."

Grinning weakly, I cup Sassy's gray muzzle. She stamps her hoof impatiently, narrowly missing my leg. *Get up and get on,* she seems to be saying, *so we can ride out of these godforsaken mountains.*

I couldn't agree with her more.

★ ★ ★

The next morning we bivouac beyond a town named Grundy.

Last night's march cost General Burbridge eight men and seven horses. They were the unlucky ones who tumbled off the mountain and could *not* be rescued. Many horses have pulled up lame from the rocky trail, and a number of soldiers are in the hospital tent with fever from the chilling rain, or broken limbs from falls.

They'll be left behind, as will Private Murphy.

It takes a while to get a fire burning with damp wood, but when it flames up, Pa has our squad circle around it. We are wet and weary, but we bow our heads in prayer, thankful that we didn't lose one of our own.

Braving the cold drizzle, Private Black, Pa, and I use our ponchos to pitch a rude tent. While Private Black fixes a meal of salt pork and corn dodgers, I check on Hambone, Sassy, Hero, and Champion.

The four horses are tethered on a picket line between two trees. We've fed them their rations of corn, but we had to leave their hay on the other side of the mountain. I know they're still hungry, so I lead them two at a time into a small meadow in the midst of the woods.

While Sassy and Champion tear hungrily at the grass, I rub each down with a rag, checking for saddle sores and chafed skin. Then I pick their feet, looking for signs of hoof rot and stone bruises. Many of the cavalrymen have eaten and fallen asleep in their makeshift shelters, their horses half-forgotten in their exhaustion. But I can't rest until I've looked out for the animals. I'll always remember Pa's words after I rode my first race: *Your horse ran his heart out for you. Least you can do is see to its care.*

As I rub Sassy, I admire Champion's strong flanks and clean lines, and my mind drifts to Woodville Farm. If Champion was one of Mister Giles's Thoroughbreds, he'd have sweet hay, clean straw, lush pastures, and a boy to brush him morning and night. For that, all he'd have to do was run races so rich men could bet on him. Pa said that we've marched over twenty-eight miles since leaving Pikesville. Our horses carried the greatest burden, yet they received no praise and scant food. I wonder how they'll they fare in a battle against the Confederates.

Captain Waite comes by, bulky and damp in his poncho. "I've heard many stories about last night's bravery, Gabriel Alexander."

I salute him smartly, but I'm too worn out to boast. "It was my duty, sir. Private Murphy was one of us. I remembered your words, sir. 'Never leave a man behind.'"

"I'm thankful for that. And it sounds as if you weren't the only one who remembered those words. You and the rest of your pa's squad did a fine job last night. Private Murphy is resting well."

"Captain, permission to ask a question."

"Permission granted." He picks up a curry comb and rubs at a smear of mud on Champion's flank.

"What will happen to the horses when we meet the Rebels at Saltville?"

Captain Waite frowns. "From any other soldier, I would say that's an odd question. From you, Gabriel, it makes perfect sense. Your love for the horses is commendable. Many Federals think of them only as transportation. I used to feel that way, too, but I've grown quite fond of Champion. To answer your question: The soldiers will likely fight on foot, and the horses will stay behind the line."

"Thank you, sir." His answer soothes me. Using a brush, I work on a stubborn spot of dirt on Sassy's coat. "Captain, have you fought Confederates before?"

"Unfortunately I have not yet seen combat. I graduated from college just this spring." He chuckles. "I studied philosophy, which prepped me well for the realities of camp life."

I have no notion of what philosophy might be, but I can tell by the jest in his voice that it has nothing to do with hardtack and leaky tents.

"Army life has been a learning experience for me—one that I could never have imagined when I was in college," he says, dropping his voice. "So every night I must study the manual on cavalry tactics." Then his tone turns solemn. "You know, don't you, Gabriel, that officers ride their mounts into battle?"

My gaze shifts to Champion. The soldiers and horses of the other regiments have all seen fighting. Only the Fifth is untried. How will we, and horses like Champion, react when faced with the blaze of gunfire and the sight of blood?

The thought makes me shudder. I attack Sassy's rump with the brush until she swishes her tail. Last night, dangling from that rope, I was more afraid than ever before in my life. Some of the white soldiers say that the coloreds are cowards. They may be right about me. Last night, if someone had given me the choice, I would have hightailed it back to Camp Nelson rather than dangle over that cliff.

And now that I've experienced marching and bivouacking, I believe that maybe next time I'll forgo the adventure and choose mucking stalls and a nice straw bed instead.

A coward? Yep, that's me.

CHAPTER TEN

Reveille blows. I roll over, bumping into Pa's back. On the other side of me, Private Black mutters the names of his sons. Last night, we slept on damp leaves, fully clothed, our bodies spooned together and covered with two blankets. The three of us were so tired that our slumber was as dreamless as that of the corpses in the dead house.

Pa stirs first. Sitting up, he tucks in his shirt and slips on his jacket. I watch him button it. "Pa," I whisper. "Do you miss Ma?"

"With all my heart."

"Captain Waite says we may face Rebels today. Are you afraid?"

"I'd be foolish not to be." He gazes down at me as he wrestles with his boots. "Last night when I had to lower you over that cliff, my fear for you almost won out over my duty as a soldier. I should have gone in your place, but I doubted the men could hold my weight. Yet knowing I put you in harm's way nearly bested me. So, yes, Gabriel, I have been afraid every moment of this march."

He clears his throat and says in his sergeant's voice, "Wake Private Black. He needs to stoke the fire and fix breakfast. I'm going to roust the men. And then you need to help feed the horses."

"Yes, Pa. I mean Sergeant Alexander."

He smiles gently and, putting on his cap, slips from the tent.

For a moment I lie still, listening to Private Black's snores. I consider Pa a courageous man. How can a man be full of fear and yet be courageous?

I hear Captain Waite talking to Pa outside the tent. "We've another hard march, over more mountain passes. Not as tough as Laurel Mountain, but challenging nonetheless. And scouts are reporting increased Confederate activity ahead. We may encounter fighting today, so make sure the squad's rifles and ammunition are dry and ready."

"Yes, Captain."

"Is Gabriel awake?"

I crawl from the tent as fast as I can and jump to my feet. When I salute, my britches fall around my knees. It's barely dawn, the mountains are hidden with fog, and the only light is from the coals of the fire.

"Private Gabriel, please ready my horse," Captain Waite orders. "After you secure your trousers," he adds with a grin.

"Yes sir." I grab the waist and hoist them back up. Captain Waite strides off, and Pa heads to a stream to fill the canteens so we can wash up. By now Private Black is awake, too, stretching and complaining about the early hour. "Even mules don't rise before the cussed sun," he grumbles.

"We might meet Rebels today!" I exclaim, my cowardly thoughts chased away by visions of a skirmish.

He pretends to sniff the wind. "Thought I could smell 'em. Now let's see, what can I fix for breakfast?"

I pat my stomach. "I'm hungry for flapjacks and bacon doused in syrup."

"How 'bout last night's corn dodgers fried in pork grease?"

"Dodgers *again?*" I pick up my saddlebag of corn. "Seems the horses get better feed than we do."

Too quickly, the sun peeks through the mist. Tents are struck, saddles are packed, and the trumpeter sounds "to horse." Since word's gone round that Confederates are likely to strike at any time, tension is high. Horses dance and riders yank reins. Sassy seems quiet in comparison. Her left front hoof is warm, and I worry that yesterday's journey has lamed her.

Sticking my toe in the stirrup, I swing into the saddle. I'm stiff and bruised, but as orders ring down the column, my blood begins to flow hot.

Rebels are ahead and Saltville is only two days away.

★ ★ ★

Clinch Mountain. Colonel Glitner. 10th Kentucky. As we saddle up the next morning, those names are on every soldier's tongue, though the words mean naught to me.

During yesterday's march, a small Rebel cavalry regiment plagued the front lines, but our brigade under Colonel Ratliff's command never heard a shot. Company B's ride was rough only due to the long hours on hard saddle seats.

Last night we camped at a farm tucked in a valley. By the time the Fifth arrived there, another Kentucky brigade led by General Hobson had already swooped like vultures upon the house and barns, cleaning out all the food from the larders and grain from the bins. The Fifth camped in a pasture on the outskirts with the rest of Ratliff's brigade, so at least there was grass for the horses.

As we ride out this morning, we pass by the farmhouse that was raided. The family's slaves are bunched by the gate, their meager bundles slung over their shoulders or balanced on their heads.

Their eyes bug as we jog past in twos, and I straighten in the saddle. Private Black rides on my left. In front of us, Private Morton has taken the place of Private Murphy, and next to him, on the left, is Private Crutcher on Whistler. Pa and Hero are in front, to the left of us.

The slave family falls into step beside us. "If black men be ridin' horses and carryin' rifles, den Jubilee must be here!" a gray-haired man calls up to us.

"It soon will be, old uncle," Private Crutcher replies.

"Then glory be to God!" the old man shouts. "C'mon, Sylvie. C'mon, Dade." He motions to the others. "C'mon and join dese soldiers marchin' to freedom!" The slaves fall into step beside us, chanting *Jubilee! Jubilee!*

My heart swells. *This is why we're fighting.*

The wagon road grows steeper, and soon the name Clinch Mountain begins to hold some meaning. After an hour of traversing switchbacks and jumping gullies, I feel like this mountain has us in its clinch, all right. But it's daytime, and the rain has slacked off to a mizzle. This climb ain't near as tough as the one over Laurel Mountain.

As we ride, Private Black keeps his gaze trained on the outcroppings of white boulders that loom over us from the steep hillsides on my right. I finally get up the nerve to ask him what he's looking for.

"Perfect spots for Rebel ambushes," he says.

"What's an ambush?" I ask, still ignorant of much of the army talk I hear.

"That's when the enemy is too scared to show his face," Private Crutcher calls over his shoulder. "The cowards hide and shoot from behind cover."

"I call it the worst way to die," Private Black adds. "A shot from an ambusher don't leave you time to get revenge—or say your goodbyes."

Turning in his saddle, Pa adds, "Captain Waite says the pesky regiment trying to keep us from reaching Saltville is the 10th Kentucky Cavalry, commanded by Colonel Giltner. They're Kentuckians who cotton to the Confederates." He shifts back to face the front. "Boys, that means we may find ourselves grappling with Kentucky slaveholders."

"Huzzah!" the soldiers around us cheer.

But a chill jitters through me, and I aim my eyes on those boulders, too.

Suddenly, sharp pops echo up the lane, far ahead of us. All talk stops. I tense, and Sassy nervously tosses her head.

More shots ring out, closer this time. Two rows in front of Pa, a cavalryman topples off his horse. An instant later, bullets rain from the boulders above us, and the riderless horse drops to his knees with a groan.

I stifle a scream.

"Find cover! Prepare to fight on foot!" The order blasts from the front of the platoon. The soldiers spur their horses into the trees to the left, crashing over rocks and into each other in their haste.

Sassy scrambles down the mountainside. I jump off, stumbling along beside her before pulling her to a stop. Pa, Black, Morton, and Crutcher have dismounted, too. I grab their horses' reins while the men dive behind outcroppings and tree trunks, grabbing wildly for their rifles.

I lead Sassy and the other horses farther into the woods, doing my best to hurry them along without starting a panic. Corporal Vaughn, also a horse holder, hastens with me. I calm the horses with soft words, trying to keep from being trampled as they bunch into each other. My breath is coming in gasps. Bullets continue to hail from the boulders beyond the road, splintering bark and pinging into the dirt, but I hear no order to fire from our side.

"Private Alexander," Corporal Vaughn dares to whisper. "What's happening?"

Before I can respond, I hear the clattering of what seems like hundreds of iron-shod hooves as a company from the 11th Michigan races up the road toward the mountaintop, pistols drawn. Their bugler trumpets, and my heart races with them.

They gallop by in a stream of puffing horses. Then it's silent for several minutes, until I again hear gunfire, shouts, and yells.

While our company waits behind cover, Corporal Vaughn and I do our best to keep the horses calm. Finally, "all clear" drifts through the forest.

Relieved, we lead the horses forward. As I watch the men rise from the shadows, it hits me: While the 11th Michigan charged forward to meet the enemy, the Fifth stayed in the brush like cowards.

Private Black strides over to get his and Crutcher's mounts. Private Morton takes his horse, his face pale under his cap. I long to talk to them about the skirmish, but their thoughts seem far away.

Pa walks solemnly toward me, rifle in his hand. When I give him Hero's reins, I ask, "Pa why didn't the Fifth go after that 10th Kentucky?"

"Because that wasn't the order."

"But ain't soldiers supposed to fight?"

Pa levels one eye at me. "Soldiers are supposed to obey orders."

"Sergeant Alexander!" Captain Waite calls from the road. "Have your squad form a detail to bury Private Huston!"

"Yes sir!" Pa responds, handing me back the reins. I lead Sassy and Hero up onto the road. In front of us a bulky mound lies in the center of the lane. The horse that was shot is dead. Blood oozes from its neck and shoulder.

Already someone has stripped it of bridle, saddle, and gear. Soldiers lead their mounts around it or step over it. No one but me pays it any mind.

I remember Jackson's words when we first visited Camp Nelson and saw the broken-down remounts: *Horses don't choose to fight, and they sure don't get no enlistment fee.*

And no glory neither, I see now. The body will be left for vultures and other varmints.

My eyes blur. I lead Sassy and Hero around the fallen horse and say a silent prayer.

The sun breaks through the clouds as Burbridge's army descends Clinch Mountain and follows Laurel Creek. The story making its way down the column is that three of Colonel Hobson's regiments dismounted to fight the 64th Virginia, sending the Rebels scattering into the hills. The Fifth hasn't been threatened again, but as we jog alongside the creek, I can't shake thoughts of that dead horse and rider from my mind.

We make it through Low Gap without any more encounters with graycoats. Saltville's only a few miles away. A fever seems to infect Pa's squad, and I'm catching it, too. Something has us riled for battle. Might be the dead comrade we buried on Clinch Mountain. Might be the salty smell of the town wafting our way. Might be the sun falling behind the hills, covering our approach.

General Burbridge must be blind to the men's eagerness, though, because after we ford the Holston River, he halts the division and orders the army to make camp. I dismount, and as Pa's squad untacks their horses, the grumbling begins.

"Why're we stoppin' now?" Private Black complains. "We need to attack Saltville while them Rebels are eatin' dinner."

"And while they're whittlin' and playin' cards," Private Crutcher joins in. "A night's delay'll just give their regiments time to regroup."

"Pa says a soldier always obeys orders," I tell them.

Private Black snorts. "Long as the order comes from Cap'n Waite, I'll follow it. But them other officers?" He hawks up a mouthful of saliva and spews it out on the ground. "Their regiments have been taunting us this whole march. Them white soldiers don't care spit about us coloreds. And I ain't plannin' on takin' a bullet for 'em neither."

"We ain't taking bullets for them," I say. "We're fighting for the slaves. Like those men at the farm that followed us—to find Jubilee."

"Ha!" Private Crutcher barks a laugh. "Only they ain't slaves no more. President Lincoln freed the Virginia coloreds long ago. They were just too scared to leave before."

"They were not too scared!" I protest. "They needed someone like us to lead them."

"Take a look, boy." Private Crutcher waves his arm around the camp. "You see 'em anymore?"

I think back, realizing I ain't seen a single one of them since we started up Clinch Mountain.

"Soon as the Rebels started firin' on us, them gutless coloreds ran back to their master's farm like frightened sheep," Private Crutcher declares. "Nope, we're fightin' for ourselves. And me, I don't aim to be buried under a pile of Virginia rocks like Private Huston."

Private Black's "Amen!" puts an end to the discussion.

When Private Crutcher leads his horse to the river to drink, Private Black draws me aside and pulls something from underneath his jacket. It's an envelope, stained and tattered as if it's traveled a long way. "Gabriel, unless them Rebels wave the white flag, we're marchin' on Saltville tomorrow. Unlike Private Crutcher, I ain't fightin' for myself. I'm fightin' for my sons so they'll have a better life than me. This letter's to them in case I..."

I glance sharply up at him. "Die? Why, you're too ornery to die, Private Black."

He leans closer, and for once there's no jest in his face. "I know something of life, Private, and I don't need no white colonel to tell me them Confederates will defend their town with every ounce of their strength. Word from Cap'n Waite is that the Fifth is goin' into combat right along with Ratliff's brigade."

This is the first I've heard of going into battle. I think of Pa and the rest of the squad, and I don't know whether to be thrilled or scared out of my britches.

"I've driven many a mule team into the South," Private Black goes on, "and I can tell you one sure thing: When them Confederates see our black faces charging 'em with rifles and bayonets, they're goin' to attack us with a vengeance. So if I die, I want my sons to know how much I love 'em. I want my sons to know I thought about 'em every step of every day."

"Yes sir," I whisper, trying to swallow the lump in my throat.

He places the letter in my hand and closes my fingers around it. "Promise on the Bible?"

I barely choke out a weak "yes."

After tomorrow, I suddenly realize, *when the Fifth marches on Saltville, none of our lives will ever be the same.*

CHAPTER ELEVEN

A rapid burst of gunfire echoes across the fog-shrouded hills. It's scarcely dawn, but the men are already up, moving about sluggishly. All have slept fitfully. As Pa walks among his squad, he tells us that the shooting is from Burbridge's skirmishers, sent ahead to sound out the enemy.

The men are quiet as they saddle their horses. I'm checking Sassy's girth when Private Crutcher leads Whistler over. "Gabriel," he says, his voice low. "I've pinned my name to my pocket." He taps a slip of paper with a name penciled on it. "If I die, don't let me rot on Rebel soil."

This time I don't protest, because I know it might be true. I nod instead, hoping I can keep all my promises. Then I glance at Pa. What if *he* should get shot?

Before we ride off, I want to tell him how proud I am of him and how much I love him. But now's not the time. He's inspecting a rifle, acting as Sergeant Alexander, not my pa.

I bend to check Sassy's leg and spy a hawk feather on the .

ground. Stooping, I retrieve it and hold it up in the misty morning light. It's a good-sized one, striped brown and white.

When Pa passes near, I reach up and tuck the quill of the feather into the chin strap that's in place over the brim of his forage cap. "So I know," is all I say in a thick voice, and he gives my shoulder a gruff squeeze.

The bugles announce it's time to mount. My guts twist as the cavalrymen swing into the saddles. I'm riding with them this time. Not as a soldier, but as a horse holder. Captain Waite gave the order on my behalf, so I didn't have to convince Pa, who would have said no.

Pa's angry about the decision. He wants his son here in camp, far from Rebel gunfire. But I don't want to be left behind. The squad has drilled and marched together for more days than I can count. These soldiers are my family now, too.

When the sun peeks over the hills, the division heads toward Saltville. We ford the Holston River, the water splashing our horses' bellies. Ahead of our company, Captain Waite rides on Champion.

This journey ain't been easy, but I've learned much. I've come to believe the captain's done his best to be a good officer, despite his scant experience and head full of philosophy. Company B will follow him wherever he leads. But like all the soldiers around me, I don't know what lies ahead. We're following the orders of our captain, who's following the orders of Colonel Wade, who's following the orders of Colonel Ratliff, who's following the orders of some general I've never laid eyes on. Here's a harsh truth: A soldier must obey as blindly as a slave.

Maybe Annabelle's right. Freedom for coloreds *is* about reading and writing. As Sassy carries me closer to Saltville, I say a prayer that Annabelle will continue to be a fine and fierce teacher. I only hope that I will see her and Ma again.

I glance at Private Crutcher, riding in front of me with his name pinned over his heart so he won't die forgotten in Rebel territory. Then I look at Private Black—his gaze straight ahead, his handsome face showing no emotion, but I know inside he's hoping with all his might that he'll live to see his sons again.

Lastly, my eyes cut to Pa and the hawk feather poking from his forage cap. As he rides toward a faceless enemy, is he thinking about Ma and their unborn babe—one he may never know? And suddenly, as Company B halts at the bottom of a hill, I discover another truth: Men *can* be courageous even when they're filled with fear.

A bugle sounds across the field. From the distance I hear Captain Waite's voice, strong and clear: "Dismount— prepare to fight—on foot!"

My last truth ain't about learning or obeying or being brave. It's the sorrowful realization that I never got a chance to tell Pa I love him.

★ ★ ★

Folks love to speak of the hardest thing they've ever experienced. Take Mister Pie and his missing eye. For him, the loss of that eye was so grand that it's become a shifting tale of truth and lies.

For me, the hardest thing is standing at the bottom of Sander's Hill holding the horses while Pa, Captain Waite, and 400 soldiers of the Fifth advance up the side. I watch them proceed in wavy rows of blue, six paces between each company, the way we drilled so many times at Camp Nelson. To the left of the Fifth marches the 12th Ohio, and on the right is the 11th Michigan. These are the regiments of the 4th Brigade.

Captain Waite, with Company B behind him, is one of the first to reach the summit. For a moment, he and Champion are silhouetted against the morning sky, and I hear his rallying cry. I strain for a glimpse of Pa or Private Black, but they're too far away. The ranks of soldiers crest the hilltop, the colors of the three regiments snapping in the wind, and then flow like a blue river over the top and disappear on the other side.

A volley of gunfire and the boom of cannons ring in the air.

My insides tighten. All I can do when the soldiers are out of sight is to soothe the horses, even though Sassy, Hambone, Whistler, and Hero are too jaded to dance.

The sun creeps above the horizon. Long hours pass.

I wait with the other horse holders staggered along the bottom of Sanders Hill. I've led my horses under a shady tree so I can rest my back on the trunk. They're hungry and they pick around at the grass, but they can't eat much. I don't dare drop the bits from their mouths in case of a hasty retreat.

The far-off sound of shooting never ceases. Patrols gallop constantly over the hill and across the river, bringing messages to and from the battlefields and camp, occasionally splitting off to relay information to the other brigades fighting west of the Holston River. No one tarries to tell us news.

All that's left is waiting and wondering.

★ ★ ★

Hours later my body still flinches with each gunshot. *Did that Rebel bullet hit Pa? Or did it find Captain Waite?*

I try and trick my mind into forgetting about the raging battle. Closing my eyes, I pretend I'm riding Aristo bareback, racing along Mister Giles's grass track. The wind pummels my cheeks as he gallops, his long legs grabbing the earth with each stride. I imagine Short Bit and Jase racing Savannah and Captain alongside us. Lord, how I miss them all! But a series of sharp pops cuts into my dreaming, and my eyes snap open. Atop the hill, I see smoke from gunpowder drift skyward, and then I hear the scream of a horse and the distant cries of men. My thoughts are once again riveted on the other side of that mountain.

Booms and cracks are also coming from the west, across Holston River. From the urgent shouts of the patrols I gather that Hanson's and Hobson's brigades are fighting the Rebels along Broddy Bottom and Little Mountain.

As the day lengthens, Union guards begin to return, driving groups of Confederate prisoners in front of them. I gape as they pass. It's the first time I've seen Rebel soldiers, and I stare, remembering tales of their fierceness in battle. But these prisoners appear defiant boys, no older than me. Their ragtag uniforms look as if they were cobbled together from their mothers' clothes trunks. One of the prisoners is a gray-haired gentleman the Union guard calls "Governor."

Then wounded Union soldiers start to stagger in from the lines. Some limp by, dragging injured legs. Some are holding their sides. Soldiers prop each other up the best they can, some using rifles as crutches. When one worn-out soldier reaches his horse, he sags against it and weeps.

A regiment surgeon and his assistants have set up a makeshift field hospital not far from where I stand. The injured are stretched on blankets spread out under a tree. I hear them call out in their misery. Scattered around them on the ground are lint, bandages, a bucket, a washbasin, and a bottle of whiskey. I wince to think that we had more medicine, supplies, and herbal remedies for the horses at Woodville Farm.

As the wounded trudge by me, I anxiously scan their faces, looking for men from Company B. I see no colored soldiers, only white men whose faces are blackened from gunpowder. Still, as they trickle past, I hear scraps of news: "Ammunition running out." "Fifth is fighting gallantly." "Soldiers falling like rain." "Rebels dug in tight on Chestnut Ridge." And finally, uttered with fear and dismay, the message "Breckenridge is on his way!"

I stop Corporal Vaughn. "Who's Breckenridge?" I ask.

"Confederate Major General Breckenridge," he replies. "Word is he's brought a detachment of five thousand to fight us."

Five thousand? My skin goes cold.

I hear the thud of hooves to our right. Mounted Yankees are trotting toward us from across the river. Most appear to be officers, although a few enlisted men, some of them bloodied, bring up the rear.

Corporal Vaughn stands upright and salutes. "That's General Burbridge," he tells me. Snapping to attention, I salute as well, hoping the general will bring news of a victory. But he and his attendants keep right on riding, their eyes toward camp. A captain peels off from the group and begins passing the word that Colonel Hobson is now in charge of the division.

I watch General Burbridge's retreating back as he canters briskly past a wagon filled with wounded soldiers. I can hear their screams and moans as the rough ground jostles the wagon bed, but the general doesn't even glance at them. He's in a hurry.

"Gabriel!" someone shouts hoarsely, and I whirl to see Private Crutcher stumbling down Sanders Hill. I hurry toward him, leading the horses, and he falls to his knees in front of me.

"Are you shot?" I ask.

He nods. His palm is clasped to his chest, and his breaths are wheezy.

"You need a surgeon!"

He shakes his head. "Help…me…on…Whistler," he croaks between scabby lips.

"But you can't ride," I protest. "You need doctoring."

Ignoring me, he crawls like a dog toward Whistler. He grabs the stirrup and slowly, his face drained from the effort, pulls himself upright. From there, I boost him into the saddle and loop the reins over the pommel. He slumps forward, one hand still on his chest, the other limply holding Whistler's mane, and gasps, "Farewell—Gabriel."

"Goodbye, Private Crutcher." I salute him, biting back the tears. Turning Whistler toward camp, I swat the horse on the rump. I watch as he trots off, Private Crutcher bobbling in the saddle. There are so many questions I wanted to ask him. Are Pa, Captain Waite, and Private Black still alive? And what of the other men in Company B?

I fear Private Crutcher has only enough life left in him to fulfill his last request—dying in the Union camp, not on Rebel soil.

"Loose horse!" a soldier shouts. Then I hear a high-pitched whinny. Dusk is settling in the hollow, but I recognize Champion's white star and gleaming black coat as he gallops down Sanders Hill.

My stomach sinks when I see that his saddle is empty and his neck is splotched with red. A soldier runs toward Champion, who bolts in the other direction, careening into a group of prisoners.

"Corporal Vaughn!" I call. "That's Captain Waite's mount. Hold these horses while I catch him."

Corporal Vaughn hurries over and takes the reins from me. I wave away several other soldiers bent on catching Champion, who has darted behind Sassy and Hero. His sides heave and his nostrils blow, but he seems relieved when I grab his rein and stroke his sweaty neck.

"You're safe now," I croon, checking his near side before walking to his far side. There's a slash on his neck, as if a saber blade sliced him, but it's not deep. "Champion, where's Captain Waite?"

I glance in the direction of Sanders Hill, which is suddenly swarming with soldiers. They spill over the summit and flow down the side, fleeing from an unseen enemy. It's grown darker, and it's hard to tell if their coats are blue or gray, but hurrahs rise up around me, so I gather they're Union.

Corporal Vaughn hurries over with the other horses, his face grim.

"Sir!" I call. "What's going on?"

"Our troops reached the crest of Chestnut Ridge, but they're out of ammunition. Colonel Ratliff has been ordered to bring the 4th Brigade back to camp. Horse holders should help all cavalrymen find their mounts."

"Yes sir." He hands me the three sets of reins before rushing off.

For what seems like forever, the returning soldiers walk, fall, roll, and are carried down the hill in chaotic spurts. Like Private Crutcher, many are severely wounded, yet they flee in panic as if the devil is after them. I spy Colonels Wade and Brisbin, who are still mounted. Their faces are weary, but they continue to aide and encourage the soldiers of the Fifth. Colonel Ratliff returns with the 12th Ohio and 11th Michigan, and gradually all of Pa's squad staggers from the battlefield to claim their horses.

All except Pa and Private Black.

Still holding Sassy, Hambone, and Hero, I frantically search for Corporal Vaughn. He's under the surgeon's tree, wrapping a bandage around a private's head.

"Sir, we need to form a detail to find Captain Waite, Private Black, and Sergeant Alexander."

"I'm sorry, Private Gabriel. There will be no detail." Corporal Vaughn keeps working, as if unable to meet my gaze. "Colonel Hobson has commanded all available soldiers to build bonfires here and along Broddy Bottom. Then we are to retreat."

"Retreat?" I'm so stunned I can hardly utter the word. "But what about those left on Chestnut Ridge? What about my pa?"

He shakes his head, and I notice that sweat has dried in tear tracks down his cheeks. He's aged ten years during this journey. "I don't know," he says, his voice so low I can barely hear him above the shouts and confusion. "But it appears we've been ordered to abandon the fight—as well as the wounded and dead."

CHAPTER TWELVE

Corporal Vaughn's words ring through my head like the trumpeter's song of retreat. *Abandon the wounded and dead.*

"But Corporal Vaughn, we can't just—"

"We have no choice!" he cuts off my protest, and I see the anguish in his reddened eyes. "We've been given our orders." He turns his back to me, ties off the wounded soldier's bandage, and then moves on to help another.

Before I can follow the corporal, Hambone's reins are wrested from my hand. "I need this horse!" a soldier barks.

"B-but sir, that's Private Black's mount," I stammer. The soldier's face is streaked with grime. His head is bare, but the epaulets on his shoulders tell me he's an officer. I'm forced to step back and let him take Hambone.

The trumpeter sounds "to horse," and the soldiers hasten to join what's left of their squads and companies. A lieutenant commandeers Sassy. I blink back foolish tears as her gray rump disappears in the dark. Then the exhausted surgeon asks for Hero so he can accompany a wagon of injured. *No,* I want to shout, *he's Pa's horse!* But I hand Hero over. I know how hard the doctor has been working all day to save as many men as he can.

Darkness falls over the valley. The regiments are mounted and moving off. I'm left standing with Champion, who's resting his muzzle on my shoulder, watching the brigades retreat. No one wants the blood-splattered, wild-eyed mount of a fallen captain. And no one cares that 1st Squad's stable hand is staying behind: a lowly horse handler who never gave an oath to the United States to obey without question.

A small detachment has remained here to gather wood for bonfires, and I listen to the soldiers talk. General Burbridge has ordered the lighting of the fires in hopes that the Rebel scouts will peer down Sanders Hill and into Broddy Bottom and be fooled into thinking that Burbridge's division is camped and waiting until morning to reassemble and attack Saltville.

As the men pass this information to each other, a few chuckle at the clever plan. If the Rebels are fooled, they won't chase after the retreating division. But others complain bitterly that General Burbridge should have stayed the course. Instead he has turned tail and run—abandoning his wounded and dead.

Step by step, I slip away from the light of the fires, leading Champion. His wound has crusted over, and the horse walks without a hitch. Patting his neck, I whisper my plan to him: *We must find Pa and the others.*

I check his girth, tighten it, and raise the stirrups for my shorter legs. Mounting, I settle in the saddle. I'm exhausted by the long day and no food, but I'm fired up, too. I aim Champion up the hillside, staying in the shadows cast by the flickering flames. He climbs steadily until we reach the top, where I halt him, unsure of what I'll find on the other side.

All I can see is the glow of a light in the window of a small building. Is it the lantern of an enemy or a friend? I can't tell from this far away, so I squeeze my heels into Champion's sides. I listen for calls from fallen soldiers, but the night is silent except for crickets and the crunch of gravel as the horse picks his way down the hill.

A few feet from the building, I stop Champion again, slip from the saddle, and make my way toward the window of the cabin. Inside, Union soldiers with bandaged legs or patched chests lie on the floor of the cramped space, while a surgeon in blue tends to them.

I tie Champion to a tree branch and approach the sagging doorway. The surgeon is crouched in one corner, holding a rag to a man's left side.

"Sir, permission to help," I announce myself.

He gives me a quick glance. "Permission granted." He nods to the soldier, who I now see is colored. "Hold this. The bullet pierced the flesh. Fortunately it went clean through, but the wound is bleeding profusely."

I step around the prone men, searching the black faces shining in the light of two lanterns, but I recognize no one from Company B. Stooping next to the surgeon, I take over for him and press the rag against the man's side. Despite the layers of dirt and gunpowder, I can see that it's a friend of

Private Black's, a soldier from 2nd Squad. "Private Lewis?" I ask.

He nods. "That you, Gabriel?"

"Yes sir."

"Am I goin' to die?"

"No sir. Surgeon says it's just a flesh wound. Private Lewis, do you know where Sergeant Alexander is?"

His face contorts. "It was bedlam on dat hill. Men was droppin' like feed sacks tossed from a haymow. Smoke was so thick I could barely see de end of my rifle."

"You never saw Sergeant Alexander or Private Black?"

"I couldn't see nothin' after de Rebels started shootin'. We was almost atop dat godforsaken mountain—Chestnut Ridge, dey called it, when dem graycoats attacked like wild animals. We would've beat 'em, 'cept we run out of shot."

"What about Captain Waite?"

"Last I know of him was when he told us to charge." He snorts. "Only how could we charge with no shot? Dem Rebels was hackin' us down like wheat in de field."

"Where was Captain Waite when you heard him give the command? On your right or left?"

"Gallopin' dat horse up de left side of de hill." Private Lewis licks his lips. "I could sure use a sip of water, Gabriel."

Keeping the rag pressed against his side, I look around for a canteen. I spot one within reach, drag it over by the strap, and give him several sips. Lewis nods toward the surgeon. "Doc's a good man. Stayed behind to carry us off dat hill. I didn't want to be found by no Rebel. I seen hate in dem Rebels' eyes, Gabriel, *pure hate.*"

His feverish words send chills through me.

Then his breathing grows shallow, and I gather he's drifted back asleep. The surgeon checks his wound. "It's quit bleeding. I'll bandage him later. He should be fine to move in the morning."

I nod.

The surgeon motions me to stand and walk with him to the doorway. "There are more wounded on Chestnut Ridge," he whispers as he wipes his hands with a bloody rag. "We moved as many as possible before it grew too dark. I heard you asking about your father and Captain Waite. It's more than possible they're still out there." He reaches down and picks up one of the lanterns. "Take this. You'll need it to find your way."

"Thank you, sir."

He points down the hill. "Tread carefully, Private. At the bottom, there's a ravine thick with brush. Only a few men fell there, and I believe we retrieved them all. The rest were gunned down as they advanced up the hill." His voice catches, and one of the soldiers cries out. I wonder how the doctor keeps his wits, surrounded by so much pain. He thrusts some bandages into a rucksack and hands it to me.

Holding the lantern high, I hurry to Champion and mount.

With the light to guide us, we plow through the brambles in the ravine and leap out the other side. As Champion climbs, I sweep the lantern back and forth, but I can make out nothing more than a jumble of rocks and low brush.

Then the beam catches a glint of metal. I pull Champion to a halt and lower the lantern. First I see a boot, then what looks like a man's leg. As my eyes adjust, more bodies come into focus. My heart jolts. We are standing at the edge of a field of bodies, all still as death. In the midst of such horror, my mind goes numb. Only one thought repeats in my mind: *How will I ever find Pa?*

Blowing nervously, Champion shies from the bodies. I rein him to the left, skirting the outside line of fallen soldiers. I have to keep my wits about me. Private Lewis recalled that Captain Waite was riding left of the ranks, so that's where I start my search.

Fewer bodies are scattered here, and my light shines on none who are alive. I say a prayer and press on, unmoved by the sight of so many lifeless souls sprawled on the ground as if tossed there by the wind. My mind goes back to my fright at the corpses in the dead house. Oh, how this journey has hardened me!

Then the lantern light falls on a soldier propped against a rock as if he dragged himself there. His slouch hat is tipped off his forehead. Could it be Captain Waite?

Jumping off Champion, I kneel next to the wounded man. I'm overjoyed to see that it is our captain, clutching his rifle as if expecting bad company. Blood is crusted on his neck.

"Captain?"

His eyelids flutter. I grab the canteen and rucksack from the saddle. I've doctored enough horses to know how to care

127

for a wound. I pull out a rag, dampen it, and dab the gash.

Captain Waite's head jerks and his eyes fly open. He stares at me in confusion.

"It's Gabriel, sir. You've a cut on your neck. I'm trying to clean it."

A weak but relieved smile replaces his pain and confusion. "I knew there was a reason I brought you along, Private Alexander." He winces. "I believe I broke my ankle, too. I left the boot on as a splint, and now it's swollen tight."

"We best leave it on until you see the surgeon."

He drinks some water while I bandage his neck. After he gathers his strength, I help him to his feet and he hops closer to Champion. Before mounting, he clings to the saddle, swaying unsteadily. "This horse carried me into battle like the purebred he is," he says, but then he shakes his head sadly. "The Rebels were entrenched behind fences and rocks. Company B fought courageously, Gabriel. But many fell." He averts his gaze from the shadowy hillside beyond us. "Did your pa make it back?"

I shake my head. "Nor Private Black."

"Last I saw them, they were side by side, waving the men forward. Soon after that they disappeared in a cloud of smoke from the gunpowder. Not far from where I was shot, I believe."

Standing on his good foot, the captain grasps the pommel with one hand and the back of the saddle with the other. I crouch down and give him a boost from behind, and he pulls himself high enough to place the toe of his good foot into the lowered stirrup. With a muffled cry, he swings his injured ankle over Champion's rump to the other side.

"Cavalry Tactics never mentioned mounting with a broken leg," he gasps.

As I lead Champion slowly down the hill, trying not to joggle the captain, I list the men from Company B who made it back to camp.

"The others will be found as soon as it's light," Captain Waite says forcefully. "General Burbridge and Colonel Ratliff will send out detachments. As hard as the Fifth fought, it's only right that all receive a proper burial."

I clear my throat. "Um, sir, the division retreated. By now, the brigades are probably climbing Clinch Mountain."

I glance over my shoulder. Captain Waite is staring down at me in astonishment. "Gabriel, I've never known you to lie. But what you say is incomprehensible."

I gather that he, like many others, doesn't understand the General's decision. "The surgeons and their assistants are the only ones who stayed behind," I say. "From what I saw on Chestnut Ridge, there aren't enough men left to gather the wounded, much less bury the dead."

Captain Waite falls silent. I believe if it was up to him, he would have defied orders and stayed behind to care for his men. But there's naught he can do with a bleeding neck and a broken ankle.

When we reach the cabin, approaching dawn is turning the horizon gray. A thick fog covers the hills and valleys. I summon the surgeon. By now, Captain Waite is slumped in the saddle, half-conscious.

"Take the captain to Governor Sander's house," the surgeon says brusquely. He takes the lantern from me and points to a brick chimney sticking up from the mist. "Officers from the 11th Michigan and 12th Ohio are being cared for there."

"Yes sir." I start off, hoping I might beg a bite of food to eat there, which lifts my spirits some. A slice of bread or cheese will rally me, and once I know the captain is well cared for, I can set off again to hunt for Pa and Private Black.

Just as we come within view of the governor's house, Champion halts, jolting Captain Waite awake. Pricking his ears, the horse spins in the direction of the surgeon's cabin. I hold my breath and listen, wondering what Champion heard.

Hoofbeats thud in the foggy distance. Then angry words drift down the hillside from the cabin. "Drag them coloreds outta there!" a gruff voice hollers.

The surgeon's voice rises in protest, but moments later the report of revolvers echoes through the hills. I startle with each shot.

"Oh my god!" the captain cries out hoarsely. "They're killing the wounded. During the battle, I heard them yell 'no quarter' but I paid them no mind. Now I realize they meant it."

Private Black's words flash in my mind like a warning: *When those Confederates see our black faces charging them with rifles and bayonets, they're going to attack us with a vengeance.*

Captain Waite stares into the fog. "I gather they aim to

kill every black soldier and their officers without mercy. That's why General Burbridge hightailed it out of here."

Clucking to Champion, I hurry him along a fence toward the house. When we trot into the yard, a Union surgeon's assistant meets us. "What's going on?" he asks.

"The Rebels are murdering the wounded." Captain Waite places his hand on his holster.

My mind reels as I think about Private Lewis back at the cabin. Did they kill him? And what about Pa and Private Black out there on the hillside with no protection?

"There's no time to waste," the assistant says hastily. "Confederate surgeons have set up a hospital at Emory and Henry College a few miles from here. They've pledged to care for the Union wounded as if they were their own. We have no choice but to believe them. We're loading the injured officers into a wagon."

Captain Waite nods. "Help me off my horse."

"Sir, don't go," I protest. "If you hurry you can meet up with your regiment. Champion can take you."

"I'll be safe, Gabriel. But your father may not be. Take Champion and ride to Chestnut Ridge before the fog lifts. See if you can find him. That's an order," he adds sternly.

"Yes sir." I salute him, sadness heavy on my chest: I may never see Captain Waite again.

The assistant and I are helping the captain off Champion just as a wagon pulled by a fresh team of horses wheels up to the porch. "Hurry!" the driver shouts. "We have to get everyone out now. Word is that Champ Ferguson and his guerrillas are killing all Union soldiers left behind."

Guerrillas. The word strikes new fear in my heart. I met guerrillas in Kentucky a while back, so I know they are renegades who have neither law nor mercy.

Captain Waite slings his arm around the assistant's shoulders. His face is flushed with fever. "Goodbye, Gabriel," he says, forcing a smile through his pain. "You've been the finest aide an officer could ask for."

"Thank you, sir. I've been honored to serve you." Supported by the assistant, the captain hops toward the wagon. He doesn't turn back, so I doubt he's heard my words.

Crack, crack, crack. This time the shots ring out from the top of Chestnut Ridge. In one swift move, I swing into Champion's saddle, gather the reins, and kick him into a gallop.

I hope it's not too late.

CHAPTER THIRTEEN

Champion gallops from the yard and into the mist. I steer him down the hill, through the brush and into the ravine. We follow the ravine to the left for a while before cantering up the mountainside.

By the time we reach the rock where I found Captain Waite, the fog is lifting, and the sun is poking through the clouds. I rein Champion to a halt and stare in stunned silence as the morning light creeps over Chestnut Ridge.

The hillside is littered with bodies: black and white, gray-clad and blue-coated, piled atop each other without thought of uniform or skin color. No one—Confederate nor Union—escaped the wrath of the bullets and balls, and hated enemies now lie side by side.

My throat grows tight. Ma was right. War is about death.

Movement along the top of the ridge reminds me I don't have time for ponderin' or prayin'.

Dismounting, I lead Champion back to the ravine and hide him in a clump of scraggly cedars. I pull the canteen and rucksack from the saddle and sling them over my shoulder. Crouching low, I run back to the bodies. I scurry around them like a rat, peering at faces. Here and there an arm stirs, a voice cries out, a leg shifts. There are plenty of soldiers—Rebel and Yankee—alive on this ridge, but many of them won't last through the day. I cringe with the knowing that I can't help them. I have to keep moving if I'm to find Pa and Private Black.

I spot Confederate stretcher bearers working their way from the summit. Ducking from sight, I pull a Rebel kepi from a dead soldier's head. I replace my blue cap with his gray and hope that with my now dirt-colored jacket the stretcher bearers will take me for a Reb. I feel like a traitor to the Union, but if it buys me time to find Pa, I don't care.

Ahead I spot a boulder jutting from the hillside. Heaped behind it, as if they were seeking protection from the bullets, are several soldiers in blue. As I scuttle toward them, I hear a gruff voice say, "Kill any Negro found alive."

I dive behind the rock and flatten myself against the ground. Shutting my eyes, I go as limp as the dead.

Footsteps crunch closer. I hear a *whump,* as if someone's turned a body over. Then a voice hollers, "The Tennesseans sure gave these bluecoats heck. Nothin' left here but buzzard food." The footsteps move away.

I squint one eye open, and my guts twist. The man's carrying a pistol in his hand as he steps over bodies. He's dressed in a butternut jacket, but I see no insignia. He's wearing blue jeans instead of Confederate gray.

Not stretcher bearers. Not soldiers. *These men with pistols are Rebel guerrillas.*

A plea for mercy followed by a gunshot tells me they're bent on revenge.

I feign death until I hear no more voices and no more shots.

But the sun is rising, and I know I have to stir soon. Every moment I lie here increases the chances that someone will find me or Champion. Every moment I lie here lessens my chances of finding Pa and Private Black alive.

Surrounded by these departed souls, it's hard to believe that's still possible. But I *have* to keep looking.

I lift my head and listen. I peer up the hill and down. Far to my left, Confederate stretcher bearers are hauling their wounded soldiers to the top of the hill where an ambulance wagon awaits. They've a job to do but won't bother with us Union soldiers until last.

Inch by inch, I drag myself to the boulder. Resting my back against it, I face downward. I move my gaze from fallen soldier to fallen soldier, searching for sergeant's stripes or a sign of life.

A breeze ruffles a sleeve. A fly buzzes against a cheek.

Then I see it—the pointy end of a brown and white striped feather. Delirious with hope, I scramble down the hill. The feather's still stuck in the brim of Pa's cap, but the cap's lying on bare ground, as if blasted off his head. I snatch it up and hold it to my chest.

He's got to be here! I dash from body to body, unmindful of the danger. And then, just beyond a tangle of brush I see three yellow stripes. *Pa!*

He's face down, his cheek scrunched in the dirt, his rifle and arm stretched in front of him as if he fell trying to reach that summit. His hair and forehead are matted with blood.

I shoo away the flies and place my ear to his lips. "Come on, Pa," I whisper, "you have to be alive."

A soft rush of air brushes my ear.

Tears spring to my eyes as I gently turn him over. He has a long gash on his head as if a bullet creased his scalp, and he moans when I move him.

"Pa, it's Gabriel." I yank the canteen and rucksack off my shoulder. I pour a little water on his face and on his wound. He tries to sit up, but I press him down. "Hush now, Pa. Guerrillas are hunting wounded coloreds," I warn. "I've got to get you out of here."

He stares up at me with startled, blood-crusted eyes as if he understands the danger. Keeping my eye on the movement to the west, I check his arms and legs, noting no other injuries.

"Do you think you can walk?"

He gives me a silent nod. Quickly, I bandage his wound. I tuck his cap in my jacket and place a Rebel kepi on his head as well. Two coloreds wearing Confederate gray caps ain't going to fool anyone for long—it just has to fool them long enough for me to get Pa on Champion.

"Did you see Private Black?" I whisper.

Pa has trouble speaking. I give him a sip from the canteen, and he finds his voice. "He...was...beside me...when I..." He flaps his hand to his left. "Over there."

Crouched furtively, I scoot from soldier to soldier, but there's no sign of Private Black, or of life. Voices from atop the ridge remind me we're running out of time.

I look toward the ravine, which seems a mile away, then glance toward the stretcher bearers. They're still working along the summit and the west side of the hill, but they seem to be moving this way. I don't see the guerrillas.

Then I hear gunshots from the direction of Governor Sander's house, and I pray Captain Waite and the other officers are long departed.

"Come on." Reaching around Pa, I help him to his feet and lead him down the hill toward the ravine. Pa leans heavily on me, both of us stumbling in our urgency to reach the cedars.

Champion greets me with a whicker.

I boost Pa into the saddle, and then untie the reins. The shooting grows nearer.

Pa clutches the pommel. Blood's pooling under the bandage on his head.

"Go," I tell him, holding up the reins. "They won't find me in the thicket."

He shakes his head. "We…go together…or not at all." He stretches out his hand to me.

Shouts ring close by, and Champion dances in place. Grabbing Pa's hand, I swing up behind the saddle and land on the horse's rump. Startled, Champion kicks out, but I nudge him hard in the sides, and he plunges from the cedars.

We don't dare head in the direction of Governor

Sander's house. I rein Champion to the east. He races along the ravine, jumping gullies and logs.

"Colored Yankees!" someone hollers.

My heart drums as loudly as Champion's hooves.

I glance over my shoulder. A handful of Rebels is charging after us, their revolvers raised. In front of me, Pa's slumped heavily. Champion's carrying two riders, and we're headed in the wrong direction. Betting money would be stacked against us, but I ain't quitting. That quick look told me those Rebels ain't ridin' Thoroughbreds, while Champion, like Aristo, was born to race and *win,* no matter what the odds.

Champion gallops gamely up the hill, and I steer him behind the cabin, trying to shake my pursuers. We reach the top of Sanders Hill and plunge down the other side. Pa's clinging tightly to the pommel, but I can feel his energy draining. To keep Pa from falling, I wrap one arm around his waist and steer Champion with the other hand as we fly up the hill. The bonfires are still smoldering, but there ain't a Union soldier in sight to come to our rescue.

I dare another look behind us. The Rebels have crested Sander's Hill. They halt as if worried a Yankee cannon might be aimed and waiting, but when they see it's all clear, they whoop like banshees and spur their horses.

Champion weaves around the fires and along the muddy path by the river. I fear he might fall, but he's sure-footed and true as his hooves grab the earth churned by departing horses and wagon wheels. Our brigade's had a night's head start, but there ain't no refuge for us here in Virginia. Our only hope is to catch up with the retreating troops.

Champion slows to a trot when we reach our camp from two nights ago. Discarded bundles, bloody bandages, cold campfires, and a dozen hastily dug graves are all that's left. I can tell by the ruts and hoofprints that Colonel Ratliff's brigade has fled across the river toward Clinch Mountain.

Champion's sides are heaving; his nostrils flare pink and his neck is lathered. I don't know how much longer the horse can carry us both.

"Gabriel, leave me," Pa whispers. "Save yourself."

"No," I say fiercely, tightening my grasp around him. "We go together or not at all. 'Sides, Pa, I've been up against guerrillas before. And this time, they ain't bestin' me."

A shrill *ki-yi-yi* sends shivers through us both.

"Run, Champion," I urge, aiming the horse toward the Holston River. "You can outrun those Rebel nags."

The short rest has given the stallion a chance to catch his wind. He races for the river and leaps into the water with such force that my kepi flies off my head. Legs reaching high, he trots across. In the distance, I see the rise of Clinch Mountain. If we can just make Low Gap, we might be able to hide in the crevices and boulders.

Champion springs up the bank and canters down the wide trail. His breathing's labored but he don't quit. The trail grows steeper and the woods thicker. I spy fresh horse droppings, and I pray we ain't far behind the 4th Brigade.

Gunshots dash my hopes. The Rebels are gaining on us.

Bullets whack the tree trunks lining the path. Pa and I hunker down on the horse's back, cringing as the shells zing over our heads. Champion stumbles, then rights himself, but I know something's wrong. Behind me, blood blooms on his rump, and his stride grows uneven.

Champion has been shot.

CHAPTER FOURTEEN

The Rebels are so close now I can hear the *huff, huff* of their mounts. "We've got them colored Yankees now!" one of the Rebels cries, the hate in his voice ringing in my ears.

I feel my innards plummet as I realize that without Champion to carry us, Pa and I ain't going to make it out of Virginia alive.

"I love you, Pa!" I shout in his ear, and if the Rebels hear, they must believe I'm daft. But Pa's slouched forward in the saddle as if unconscious, for which I'm grateful. At least he won't see the rage in those guerrillas' eyes when they kill us.

Champion slows to a lurching trot. I hold tight around Pa's waist and wait for a bullet to knock us off the horse's back.

A deafening volley fills the air. But the gunfire's coming from Low Gap. And the bullets are kicking up dirt in front of those Rebels, not us!

Champion startles, tossing me sideways, and I scramble to hang on. A trumpet blasts, and two dozen cavalrymen gallop toward us from Clinch Mountain. I see from the colors it's a company from the 11th Michigan.

When Champion stops, I lose my grip and fall with a thud by his hind legs. I jump up, but I'm barely in time to catch Pa and lower him to the ground. I kneel beside him. His eyes are shut and his bandage is soaked with blood, but he's still breathing.

The cavalrymen charge past us with whoops and hollers. The guerrillas have swung wide and are racing to distance them. The company's surgeon rides up and dismounts.

Standing on wobbly legs, I salute him. "Thank you, sir!" I croak through cracked lips.

"At ease, Private." He pulls a rucksack from his saddle and bends to look at Pa.

"Will he be all right?" I ask.

"With good care."

I hobble over to Champion. His legs are splayed, his sides heave, and his head hangs as he blows air in and out of his nostrils like a bellows. The wound on his hindquarters oozes blood. "Sir, may I use your canteen and antiseptic?" I ask the surgeon. "It's for my horse."

I expect him to scoff and refuse, but he nods without looking up. "You did a fine job bandaging this sergeant, so I believe you can handle your mount."

I pour water from the canteen into Pa's cap and give Champion a sip of water. Then I soak my jacket and rub it over his neck and chest to cool him off. With the last of the water, I cleanse the gash. The horse cocks his leg as if it hurts, but I probe gently with my fingers and determine that the bullet only grazed the flesh. I pour a little of the antiseptic over the wound and hand the bottle back to the surgeon. By the time the cavalrymen ride back, Champion's breathing has evened and Pa's sitting up.

The soldiers are grinning mightily. "Scared them varmints right back to Saltville," a corporal brags. I salute the captain in charge.

"You two from the Fifth?" he asks.

"Yes sir. This is my— I mean, this is Sergeant Alexander of Company B."

"Captain Waite's company?"

"Yes sir. Captain Waite broke his ankle. He's in the hands of Confederate surgeons. And sir, thank you for coming to our aid."

"Our pleasure." The captain scowls. "Sorry to hear about Waite. Hope those Rebel doctors take good care of him. Colonel Ratliff didn't agree with General Burbridge's order to leave," he adds. "We fought side by side on that hill with you men of the Fifth. No one should have been left behind."

The other riders murmur in agreement.

"Colonel Ratliff ordered us to stay behind and protect stragglers. We were glad to do what we could." The captain grins. "Although you were the first being pursued by such a ragtag band. We've been itching all morning for a good skirmish."

I'm mighty glad someone enjoys fighting. Me, I've had enough for a lifetime.

The captain straightens in his saddle, ready to be on his way. "Sir," I call, "did you happen to find a Private Black from Company B this morning?"

"Not that I know of." He shakes his head. "Scant few survivors have come by here, but we're under orders to wait out the day, just in case. I'll send a detail to escort you and Sergeant Alexander to your regiment. Colonel Ratliff's brigade should be camping on the other side of Clinch Mountain tonight. We've an extra mount for your pa. Do you think your horse can make it?"

"I won't leave him behind!" I declare.

"Whoa, son." He holds up his palm. "I'm not asking you to leave him."

I lace my fingers through Champion's mane. "He'll make it. I'll lead him the whole way if need be."

A cavalryman rides up with a horse trailing behind him. It's Hero! "That's my pa's mount," I tell them.

The surgeon grins as he takes Hero's reins and hands them to me. "Sergeant Alexander's horse helped me lead a wagon of wounded to safety. He's a fine animal."

It takes three of us to boost Pa into the saddle. But once he's seated on Hero, he attempts to sit tall. "I'm ready," he says.

It's a long, slow walk over Clinch Mountain. By the time the detail from 11th Michigan leads Pa and me into the 4th Brigade's camp, it's past dark. Several white soldiers rise from their fires to meet us. They help Pa off Hero and take us to where the Fifth have bivouacked. As I walk the horses around the campfires, I notice that the lines of the white and black regiments have blurred. Soldiers of the 11th Michigan, the 12th Ohio, and the 5th Colored Cavalry are seated together, talking of the battle.

When we reach Company B, a grand hurrah rings out. The regiment surgeon and his assistant escort Pa to the hospital tent. A lieutenant sitting on a rock outside the tent limps over to me. His arm is in a sling. "What happened to Captain Waite?" he asks. "His company was in front of ours on that ridge. Seems his men got hit the worst."

"He's a prisoner," I tell him. "Broke his ankle. Confederate surgeons took him to a hospital. I've brought his horse."

The lieutenant jerks his thumb toward a tree on the other side of the hospital tent, where a dozen sentries stand guard around soldiers squatting beside a fire. "We've got Rebel prisoners to exchange. I'll petition Colonel Brisbin on Captain Waite's behalf. Care for his horse until he returns."

"Yes sir—and thank you, sir."

"You did well, Private Gabriel," he says. "All the soldiers of the Fifth did well. I am proud to have been part of this regiment." The moment he strides off, I realize who he is: Lieutenant Wagoner, the guard who called me a guttersnipe and tried to toss me out of Camp Nelson when I first arrived.

I lead the two horses to the outskirts of camp, where the company's mounts are picketed in a field. I strip off Champion's and Hero's tack and rub them down. Corporal Vaughn brings me two nose bags of corn. As soon as

Champion is cool, I strap on one of the bags and let him eat, which he does in great, gulping bites. I gather he'll be just fine.

"Any word of Private Crutcher?" I ask Corporal Vaughn as I strap a nose bag on Hero. The corporal's wire glasses are crooked, and melancholy is etched on his face.

"We buried him by the Holston River. Lieutenant Rhodes said a prayer."

I nod sadly, remembering those graves we passed. "And Private Black?" I ask hesitantly, afraid to know the answer.

He shakes his head. "I checked all the wagons, hospital tents, and ambulances. He's not with the dead or the wounded."

"I couldn't find him on Chestnut Ridge, neither," I say, my voice cracking.

"I've been listing the wounded, dead, and missing," Corporal Vaughn says, holding up a ledger. "It's a horrible accounting. I'm glad you and your pa made it, Gabriel," he adds. "And I'm sorry I didn't stay behind to help."

"You had orders to follow."

"Yes. Orders." He sighs and, turning slowly, shuffles off into the night, his shoulders bowed. I wonder how so young a man will bear such a heavy burden.

When Hero and Champion are settled, I search among the other horses, finally finding Sassy tethered alone. The officer who rode her left her saddled and dirty. Her ears prick when she sees me, and then flatten again. *Where have you been?* her eyes seem to ask.

I check her hoof, which has cooled, and feel a pinch of

gratitude that she and most of our horses survived. I pull off the saddle and rub her down, too. But before I can finish, exhaustion and sorrow overwhelm me. Resting my head against Sassy's sweat-crusted neck, I break into sobs, grieving over those lost in battle.

When my tears are spent and Sassy is fed, I find Pa in front of the fire by the hospital tent. He's leaning against a tree trunk, his legs stretched toward the warmth. His cap is beside him, the hawk feather bent, and his head is freshly bandaged. Pain and weariness are reflected in his gaze. I sit beside him, pull up my knees, and wrap my arms around my dirty trouser legs.

Private Morton brings us plates of beans and salt pork. Silently, I dip my spoon into the beans. Though I've not eaten for a day and a night, I can barely swallow.

"Corporal Vaughn said that Private Crutcher was buried beside the Holston," I say as we eat. "I saw him come off the battlefield. I knew he didn't have long to live, but Pa, he did *not* want to be buried in enemy territory."

"I believe Private Crutcher's soul will rest easy. He would've been glad to know that Union soldiers dug his grave and said a prayer over him."

"I hope so." I sigh. "And there's no sign of Private Black." I tap the pocket inside my jacket. "He entrusted me with a letter to his sons." My lower lip begins to quiver. "In case...in case he..."

Pa wraps one arm around my shoulder. "Go ahead and cry, son." He nods at the soldiers clustered around the fire. They all bear the marks of battle—bandaged legs, arms in slings, bound ribs—and they're staring blindly into the flames with bloodshot eyes. "You won't be the first to shed tears, or the last."

I lean against his chest, but this time the tears won't fall. "I failed Private Black."

"You didn't fail anyone," Pa says. "You looked as long as you dared. We can still hope he isn't among the dead. So from this moment on, when we think of Private Black, we'll picture him striding down the lane toward his home."

I suck in a breath. "You mean deserting the army? He could be shot for that."

"Not deserting. He was too honorable for that. No, I mean let's think of him striding down that lane, heading home to those boys he loves so dear."

Closing my eyes, I picture the scene. Private Black with a face-splitting grin as Joe and Ben fall into his arms.

Pa's right. Seeing my friend that way chases away the notion of him lying on that battlefield.

"Pa, I don't want to fight anymore," I say quietly, my words for his ears only. "I don't want to lose another friend like Private Black or Private Crutcher ever again. In truth…" I hesitate, afraid to tell him of my feelings.

But he squeezes my shoulder, urging me to go on.

"In truth, before we went into battle, I called myself a coward. Now I know it's true. When we get back to Camp Nelson, I'm taking off my soldier's uniform. I'm sorry, Pa, but I've decided I'll muck stalls forever before marching again."

I'm surprised when Pa laughs instead of scolds. "Why,

that ain't being a coward, Gabriel. Look around at these wounded men. Do you think any of them are staring into the fire thinkin' excitedly about their next battle? Not on your life. Like me, their minds are on their wives and homes. Your ma's face is all I see right now. So *I* believe you should call yourself a hero. Who risked his life and stayed behind to rescue Captain Waite and me when our own general turned coward?" He gestures toward the soldiers in the camp. "None of these men here did."

"They'd already risked their lives on Chestnut Ridge," I say. "'Sides, they had to follow General Burbridge's orders."

"Burbridge?" Pa snorts. "The men told me that when our brave general knew we were losing, he ran to save his own skin. I've come to believe your ma's right, Gabriel. This war ain't about victory or defeat or freedom for coloreds. It's about death. The Rebels may believe they won, but as I charged up Chestnut Ridge, I shot soldiers clad in gray and watched them fall alongside our own. I'd say that tonight there are just as many Confederates as Union grieving for their dead and wounded."

I frown, my head muddled about heroes and cowards, victories and defeats. Too much has happened since we marched from Camp Nelson. The only thing I do know for sure is that, as far as I can figure, the battle at Saltville did nothing to bring slaves closer to Jubilee.

On the other side of the fire, a lone soldier plays a tune on his harmonica, and I recognize "Amazing Grace." He plays softly as one soldier starts to sing, then a few others chime in.

Amazing Grace, how sweet the sound
That saved a wretch like me....

Soon all the soldiers—colored and white—join in. Their voices fill the meadow and the night sky, and chills travel up my spine as the words swirl around me.

I once was lost but now am found,
Was blind, but now I see.

Just then, in the middle of all the singing, I realize something else. I sit up. "Pa, remember when you told me that the horses would bring me—bring *us*—to freedom?"

Pa looks at me curiously. The flames from the burning logs heats my face like a fever as I try to explain. "Well, I finally realized you're right. Mister Giles wrote in his letter that we could come back to Woodville anytime. When you and the Fifth don't need me anymore, I'm going back there with Ma and the new baby. I've been missin' Short Bit, Jase, and Tandy—even Old Uncle—like all heck! And with me riding and Jackson training, Mister Giles's Thoroughbreds will be unbeatable on the racetrack. I've already got two hundred dollars in the bank, and with a few more wins, I might even be able to earn enough to buy Aristo."

Pa stays very quiet so I can't tell what he's thinking.

"When this war's over," I rush on in my excitement, "the North and South will both need horses. After you're mustered out of the army, we'll buy our own farm—Ma, you, me, and Annabelle if she wants. A farm with sweet grass and a few mares so Aristo can sire a whole herd of fine Thoroughbreds! Maybe we'll even head out west, where land is cheap."

When I pause to take a breath, I swear I can see those horses in the firelight: strong steeds galloping free, their manes blowing, their nostrils flaring as they race across the pasture of flickering flames. This journey has been long and hard and full of death, but somehow it hasn't brought me to an end. It's led me—led *all* of us—to a beginning.

"Do you see them, Pa?" I whisper. "*Our* horses on *our* farm? Or am I dreamin'?"

"You ain't dreamin'." Pa's arm tightens around my shoulder as he gazes into the fire, a smile slowly creasing his face. "I see them, Gabriel. I see those horses, too."

AFTERWORD

Gabriel and his family and Captain Waite are fictional characters, but the story of the Fifth United States Colored Cavalry and the battle of Saltville and the Saltville Massacre is real. The following characters in the story are based on real soldiers who fought at the battle.

UNION:

General Stephen G. Burbridge: Relieved of command several months after the defeat at Saltville.

Colonel Charles Hanson: Wounded in action; Confederate surgeons saved him from being murdered by Rebel guerrillas.

General Hobson: Commanded a brigade of Kentucky mounted infantry and cavalry at the battle of Saltville.

THE 4TH BRIGADE

Colonel Robert Ratliff: Originally commander of the 12th Ohio; also placed in command of the 11th Michigan and the Fifth Colored Cavalry for the battle of Saltville.

THE FIFTH REGIMENT:

Colonel James Brisbin: Wrote a letter after the battle proclaiming the courage of the soldiers of the Fifth.

Colonel James F. Wade: Promoted based on his performance at the battle of Saltville.

COMPANY B:

Private Joseph Black: Listed as missing in action after the battle of Saltville.

Private George Lewis: Wounded in the left side during the battle of Saltville. Listed as murdered by the enemy.

Private Andrew Crutcher: Missing in action after the battle of Saltville; later identified as killed in action.

Corporal George Vaughn: Promoted to quarter sergeant after the battle of Saltville.

CONFEDERATE:

Champ Ferguson: Rebel guerrilla; one of several men who were believed to have murdered wounded soldiers of the Fifth. Hanged (for other war crimes) on October 20, 1865.

General John C. Breckenridge: Arrived in Saltville with a force of cavalry after the Union army departed.

THE HISTORY BEHIND GABRIEL'S JOURNEY

Black Soldiers in the Civil War

By the end of the Civil War, 178,975 soldiers had served in the United States Army as members of the U.S. Colored Troops. Another 9,695 African American men served in the U.S. Navy. There were 135 infantry regiments, 7 cavalry regiments, 12 regiments of heavy artillery and 10 batteries of light artillery. Black soldiers fought in thirty-nine major battles. Some of them served as officers, surgeons, and chaplains. More than a dozen black soldiers received the Medal of Honor after the war. Sergeant William H. Carney was the first African American to be awarded this medal. He was honored for carrying the Union flag to safety despite being shot in the head, arm, leg and chest.

Sergeant William H. Carney

It was not easy for most blacks to become soldiers. Thousands of slaves risked punishment and death when they ran away to enlist. Some were shot by Confederate soldiers. Others were hunted and caught by their angry masters. Kentucky slave Elijah Marrs wrote: "...we were in the recruiting office in the city of Lexington.... By twelve o'clock the owner of every man of us was in the city hunting his slaves..."

Racism in the Union Army

When the Civil War began in April 1861, many African Americans wanted to join the fight. But the U.S. War Department did not allow blacks to enlist. Even though many white Northerners were against slavery, they did not feel that blacks were skilled or brave enough to become soldiers. Others worried about giving weapons to blacks. And most Northerners believed that the war was being fought to restore the Union, not to free the slaves.

The first African Americans to serve in the army were slaves who ran away from plantations or from Confederate troops to seek refuge in Union army camps. They were considered to be "contrabands," or "property of the enemy." These men were used as cooks, drivers, and laborers. Union troops soon realized the value of these workers. During the summer of 1861, the United States Congress passed the first Confiscation Act. This allowed Northern armies to seize any slaves helping the Confederate cause.

On January 1, 1863, the Emancipation Proclamation freed slaves in most of the states fighting against the Union. Border states such as Kentucky and Maryland were not affected if they declared loyalty to the Union. At the same time, the Union army was given the power to recruit slaves for labor, not for military fighting.

Demand for soldiers caused this policy to change. The war had been dragging on, and the number of white volunteers and recruits was growing smaller. The Northern troops needed reinforcements, so the army gradually looked to African Americans

Union officers with "contrabands"

to fill the ranks. In May 1863, the U.S. War Department set up the Bureau of Colored Troops. Its job was recruiting black soldiers. Special posters promised money and freedom to "colored" men who joined the army.

In spite of the desperate need for soldiers, though, most white Northerners did not want to fight side by side with black men. From the beginning, African American soldiers were placed in their own separate units. Nearly all troops were led by white officers. By the end of the war, there were only about eighty black officers among the nearly 190,000 who served.

Pay for black soldiers was not equal to pay for whites. In 1863, the standard monthly salary for a white enlisted soldier was thirteen dollars, plus a three-dollar clothing

TO COLORED MEN!

FREEDOM,
Protection, Pay, and a Call to Military Duty!

On the 1st day of January, 1863, the President of the United States proclaimed FREEDOM to over THREE MILLIONS OF SLAVES. This decree is to be enforced by all the power of the Nation. On the 21st of July last he issued the following order:

PROTECTION OF COLORED TROOPS.

"WAR DEPARTMENT, ADJUTANT GENERAL'S OFFICE,
WASHINGTON, July 21.

"*General Order*, No. 233.

"The following order of the President is published for the information and government of all concerned:—

EXECUTIVE MANSION, WASHINGTON, July 30.

"'It is the duty of every Government to give protection to its citizens, of whatever class, color, or condition, and especially to those who are duly organized as soldiers in the public service. The law of nations, and the usages and customs of war, as carried on by civilized powers, permit no distinction as to color in the treatment of prisoners of war as public enemies. To sell or enslave any captured person on account of his color, is a relapse into barbarism, and a crime against the civilization of the age.

"'The Government of the United States will give the same protection to all its soldiers, and if the enemy shall sell or enslave any one because of his color, the offense shall be punished by retaliation upon the enemy's prisoners in our possession. It is, therefore, ordered, for every soldier of the United States, killed in violation of the laws of war, a rebel soldier shall be executed; and for every one enslaved by the enemy, or sold into slavery, a rebel soldier shall be placed at hard labor on the public works, and continued at such labor until the other shall be released and receive the treatment due to prisoners of war.

"'ABRAHAM LINCOLN.'"

"'By order of the Secretary of War.

"'E. D. TOWNSEND, Assistant Adjutant General.'"

That the President is in earnest the rebels soon began to find out, as witness the following order from his Secretary of War:

"WAR DEPARTMENT, WASHINGTON CITY, August 3, 1863.

"SIR: Your letter of the 3d inst., calling the attention of this Department to the cases of Orlo H. Brown, William H. Johnston, and Wm. Wilson, three colored men captured on the gunboat Isaac Smith, has received consideration. This Department has directed that three rebel prisoners of South Carolina, if there be any such in our possession, and if not, three others, be confined in close custody and held as hostages for Brown, Johnston and Wilson, and that the fact be communicated to the rebel authorities at Richmond.

"Very respectfully your obedient servant,

"EDWIN M. STANTON, Secretary of War.

"The Hon. GIDEON WELLES, Secretary of the Navy."

And retaliation will be our practice now—man for man—to the bitter end.

LETTER OF CHARLES SUMNER,

Written with reference to the Convention held at Poughkeepsie, July 15th and 16th, 1863, to promote Colored Enlistments.

BOSTON, July 13th, 1863.

"I doubt if, in times past, our country could have expected from colored men any patriotic service. Such service is the return for protection. But now that protection has begun, the service should begin also. Nor should relative rights and duties be weighed with nicety. It is enough that our country, aroused at last to a sense of justice, seeks to enrol colored men among its defenders.

"If my counsels should reach such persons, I would say: enlist at once. Now is the day and now is the hour. Help to overcome your cruel enemies now battling against your country, and in this way you will surely overcome those other enemies hardly less cruel, here at home, who will still seek to degrade you. This is not the time to hesitate or to higgle. Do your duty to our country, and you will set an example of generous self-sacrifice which will conquer prejudice and open all hearts.

"Very faithfully yours,

"CHARLES SUMNER."

Civil War recruitment poster

allowance. Black soldiers were paid only ten dollars a month, and three dollars was deducted from their salary for clothing. In August 1864, Congress passed a law making soldiers' pay equal for all men who were free when the war began. It wasn't until March 1865 that Congress finally passed a law giving all black soldiers pay equal to that earned by whites.

African American soldiers were often assigned "fatigue duty." This meant that they worked eight to ten hours a day digging ditches, handing out rations, unloading supplies, repairing bridges, and burying the dead. Finally, in June 1864, the War Department issued an order forbidding camp commanders to assign more fatigue duty to black soldiers than to whites. But the new order was hard to enforce.

Camp Nelson, Kentucky

Camp Nelson was a Union military camp located south of Lexington, Kentucky. Covering over 800 acres, the grounds held more than 300 buildings, including the Soldiers Home, a prison, a hospital, a blacksmith shop, a bakery, corrals, and a laundry. Set up as a supply depot for Union troops fighting in Tennessee, the facility also provided and trained horses and mule teams.

In the Conscriptive Act of February 1864, President Lincoln authorized the use of black troops for the war effort. Kentucky African Americans, free and slave, poured into Camp Nelson to enlist. On July 25 alone, 322 black recruits joined up. The government paid freedmen like

Gabriel's father an enlistment fee. Slaves who became soldiers were given their freedom, and some of their former masters were paid three hundred dollars.

Camp Nelson soon became the third-largest recruiting and training center for black soldiers in the country. From November 1864 to April 1865, almost 5,400 Kentucky slaves and freemen enlisted there.

For many of the black recruits, Camp Nelson was their first experience with freedom. These men—and the women and families who came with them—had a powerful desire to attend school. On July 19, Reverend John G. Fee established the Camp Nelson School for Colored Soldiers. "I find them manifesting an almost universal desire to learn; and that they do make rapid progress," Reverend Fee wrote of his scholars.

During late summer and fall of 1864, when Gabriel and Annabelle were at Camp Nelson, school attendance was high. In one day, an average of 60 soldiers, 30 boys, and 40 young women and girls went to class. After six weeks of

Colored school at Camp Nelson

working in the camp, Reverend Fee wrote that he had "a very excellent school room—a good supply of slates books &c." He also had thirteen eager volunteers like Annabelle to help him teach.

Fredericksburg, VA, troops filling canteens, 1864

Horses During the Civil War

During the Civil War, both the Confederate and Union armies depended heavily upon horses. One of Camp Nelson's biggest responsibilities was supplying horses and mules for the Union troops fighting in Tennessee. The animals were needed to pull wagons, cannons, and ambulances to and from battlegrounds. The horses also carried cavalry soldiers and officers into battle.

About 1.5 million horses and mules died during the Civil War. (Approximately 700,000 soldiers died.) One Union officer reported that Rebel sharpshooters had killed or wounded 500 horses in one day. But not all the animals died in battle. Many of them died from disease, poor food (or no food), poor care, and overwork. Major William Jennens, a Union cavalryman, wrote: "From the 16th of May to the 19th horses were without feed.... During this time we traveled thirty-five miles; the last five we traveled at a gallop causing horses to give out by the dozens."

The Union Colored Cavalry

During the Civil War, the Bureau for Colored Troops recorded only seven black cavalry regiments. In June 1864, officers from Camp Nelson began selecting recruits for the Fifth Colored Cavalry (Gabriel's regiment). Nearly all of the recruits were former slaves. The officers, like the fictional Captain Waite, were white men. Before the regiment was completely organized, it was sent to Saltville, Virginia. Colonel James S. Brisbin traveled with the Fifth as they marched from Kentucky to Virginia.

"On the march the colored soldiers, as well as their white officers, were made the subject of much ridicule and many

Federal cavalry column,
Rappahannock River, VA, 1862

insulting remarks by the white troops," Colonel Brisbin reported. "These insults as well as jeers and taunts that they would not fight, were borne by the colored soldiers patiently..."

The Fifth lost 114 men (out of 400) and four officers during the battle. Afterward, Colonel Brisbin reported: "Of this fight I can only say that men could not have behaved more bravely. I have seen white troops fight in twenty-seven battles and I never saw any fight better."

Saltville battlefield, 1864

The Battle of Saltville, Virginia

The town of Saltville was the scene of a fierce battle between the North and the South. During the Civil War, the troops needed salt for many purposes. It was used for tanning leather shoes, harnesses, holsters, and saddles. Horses required salt in their diet. And since there was no refrigeration, beef and pork were salted to be preserved as food for the troops.

The Saltville mines and saltworks were major suppliers of salt for the Confederate armies. The Saltville pots were kept boiling throughout the war, manned by slaves twenty-four hours a day. The mines and saltworks produced thousands of bushels of salt every day.

On October 2, 1864, 5,200 Union soldiers from Eastern Kentucky and Camp Nelson, including the newly formed Fifth U.S. Colored Cavalry, attacked Saltville. The day-long fight was a Confederate victory. Many of the Union soldiers were killed, wounded, or captured.

The Saltville "Massacre"

During the Civil War the North and the South agreed to rules stating that captured soldiers were to be held as prisoners of war. When the war ended, the prisoners would be exchanged. However, the Confederate army considered black soldiers as runaway slaves. They also labeled the white officers who commanded black soldiers—like Captain Waite—as criminals because they were helping the "runaways." Jefferson Davis, President of the Confederate States of America, sent out a proclamation declaring that captured officers of black regiments were to be "put to death or be otherwise punished" and the men serving under them were to be hanged or returned to slavery.

Following the battle of Saltville, Confederate troops killed a number of wounded and captured black troops after they had surrendered. According to oral history, the bodies were buried in a nearby sinkhole. Historians disagree on the number of black soldiers "missing in action" after this battle. Estimates range from a dozen to one hundred and fifty. The killings later came to be known as the "Saltville Massacre."

When Confederate General Robert E. Lee heard of the massacre, he declared that the officers responsible should be arrested and brought to trial. It wasn't until the war was over that a Confederate guerrilla fighter named Champ Ferguson was arrested and charged with murdering fifty-three soldiers. While he was not convicted of killing the black soldiers, he was found guilty of robbery and murder. Ferguson was hanged in October 20, 1865, slightly over a year after the battle of Saltville.

Each year on October 2, a dedication and memorial service is held at the Saltville Battleground to honor the black soldiers who died in 1864.

Note: The quotes from Reverend John G. Fee were obtained from *Camp Nelson, Kentucky*. The quote from Elijah Marrs came from *Life and History of Elijah P. Marrs*. The quote from Colonel James S. Brisbin was found in *The War of the Rebellion: A Compilation of the Official Records of the Union and Confederate Armies*, Series I, Vol. XXXIX. Government Printing Office, Washington: 1892. The quote from Jefferson Davis appears in *Till Victory is Won*. The quote from Major Jennens is from "The Expendable Horse in the Civil War."

Special thanks to Robert A. Niepert, Civil War re-enactor and cavalryman, Lieutenant Colonel 3rd Battalion, Hardy's Brigade, Florida; Dr. Stephen McBride, Director of Interpretation and Archaeology, Camp Nelson Civil War Heritage Park; and David Brown, whose great-great-grandfather Samuel Truehart was a soldier in the Fifth United States Colored Cavalry.

BIBLIOGRAPHICAL NOTE

To RESEARCH AND WRITE GABRIEL'S JOURNEY, I read many books, articles, and online information. The following sources were especially helpful:

BOOKS

Cooke, Philip St. George. *The 1862 U.S. Cavalry Tactics.* Stackpole Books, PA: 2004.

Higginson, Thomas Wentworth. *Army Life in a Black Regiment.* Corner House Publishers, Massachusetts: 1971.

Kent, William B. *A History of Saltville.* Commonwealth Press, Inc. Radford, Virginia: 1955.

Lucas, Marion B. *A History of Blacks in Kentucky: From Slavery to Segregation, 1760–1891.* Kentucky Historical Society: 2003.

Lucas, Scott J. "High Expectations: African Americans in Civil War Kentucky." *Negro History Bulletin:* Jan/Dec. 2001.

Marrs, Elijah P. *Life and History of the Reverend Elijah P. Marrs.* Louisville, KY: 1885.

Marvel, William. *The Battles for Saltville.* H. E. Howard, Inc., Lynchburg, VA: 1992.

Mays, Thomas D. *The Saltville Massacre.* Ryan Place Publishers, Inc. Fort Worth, TX: 1995.

Mettger, Zak. *Till Victory is Won: Black Soldiers in the Civil War.* Puffin: 1997.

Miller, Francis Trevelyan. *The Cavalry: The Photographic History of the Civil War.* Castle Books, New York: 1957.

Murphy, Jim. *The Boys' War: Confederate and Union Soldiers Talk about the Civil War.* Clarion Books, New York: 1990.

Niepert, Robert A. "The Expendable Horse in the Civil War." *www.floridareenactorsonline.com*

Niepert, Robert. A. "The Cavalryman's Accoutrements." *www.floridareenactorsonline.com*

Ray, Delia. *Behind the Blue and Gray: The Soldier's Life in the Civil War.* Puffin: 1996.

Sears, Richard D. *Camp Nelson, Kentucky: A Civil War History.* The University Press of Kentucky: 2002.

Smith, John David, ed. *Black Soldiers in Blue: African American Troops in the Civil War Era.* University of North Carolina Press: 2002.

Wilson, Keith P. *Campfires of Freedom: The Camp Life of Black Soldiers during the Civil War.* The Kent State University Press, Ohio: 2002.

WEBSITES

www.campnelson.org

http://mywebpages.comcast.net/5thuscc/index.htm
(This is the website of David Brown, whose great grand-
father was Samuel Truehart, a Kentuckian who mustered in
at Camp Nelson on September 12, 1864, and was placed in
Company E of the Fifth Colored Cavalry. Brown has carefully researched the battle and its aftermath.)

www.saltville.com

www.vahistory.org "The Horse: A Silent Hero of Our History"

The following books will help you learn more about a
soldier's life during the Civil War:

Black, Wallace B. *Slaves to Soldiers: African-American Fighting
Men in the Civil War.* Franklin Watts, NY: 1998.

Brooks, Victor. *African Americans in the Civil War.* Chelsea
House Publishers, Philadelphia: 2000.

Corrick, James A. *Life among the Soldiers and Cavalry.* Lucent
Books, Inc., CA: 2000.

Ford, Carin T. *African American Soldiers in the Civil War.*
Enslow Publishers, Inc., NJ: 2004.

Mettger, Zak. *Till Victory is Won: Black Soldiers in the Civil
War.* Puffin: 1997.

Wisler, G. Clifton. *When Johnny Went Marching: Young Americans Fight the Civil War.* HarperCollins, NY: 2001.

ABOUT THE AUTHOR

ALISON HART enjoys writing about history and horses, two of her favorite subjects. "I'd love to go back in time," she says, "and meet people like Gabriel who followed their dreams, no matter what the hardships." Researching GABRIEL'S HORSES took her to the Bluegrass region of Kentucky and its rich Thoroughbred racing and Civil War history. She soon realized that the suspenseful story of Gabriel and his family wouldn't fit in one book. The result was the Racing to Freedom trilogy: GABRIEL'S HORSES, GABRIEL'S TRIUMPH, and GABRIEL'S JOURNEY.

Ms. Hart, a teacher and author, has written more than twenty books for children and young adults. Many of her titles—including ANNA'S BLIZZARD, an IRA Teacher's Choice and WILLA Finalist, and SHADOW HORSE, an Edgar Nominee—feature horses. Her historical mystery FIRES OF JUBILEE is also set at the time of the Civil War.